"BUT I NEVER ASKED FOR SPECIAL TREATMENT . . ."

Paisley laughed out loud. "Ask? Meg is so excited about you, she spared you all the pain. Don't be dumb—do you think every girl does magazine covers her first week on the job? Or a fashion show like this? Meg is treating you like a queen, and you don't even know it!"

Kelly squirmed. "Knock it off, Paisley—I'm not stupid. I just didn't realize what Meg has done for me."

"I'll say you didn't."

With a shock, Kelly realized Paisley was jealous. Why hadn't she realized it before? And what could she do about it now?

Bantam Books in the Kelly Blake, Teen Model Series

•••••••••2•••••••••
KELLY BLAKE
TEEN MODEL
•••••••••••••••••••••••

Rising Star

Yvonne Greene

BANTAM BOOKS
TORONTO • NEW YORK • LONDON • SYDNEY • AUCKLAND

RL 6, IL age 12 and up

RISING STAR
A Bantam Book / September 1986

*Setting of back cover photograph of Kelly Blake in the soda shoppe courtesy
of Antique Supermarket.*

ISBN 0-553-25639-4

Published simultaneously in the United States and Canada

PRINTED IN THE UNITED STATES OF AMERICA

O   0 9 8 7 6 5 4 3 2 1

Rising Star

One

"It was humiliating—the entire boys' cross-country team was watching while Coach Hayes made me do thirty extra sit-ups after practice today." Kelly Blake shook the tangles out of her damp hair and reached for her hairbrush.

"It doesn't sound like much of a Saturday, but what's so humiliating about that?"

Kelly's wide blue-green eyes grew even wider as she stared at her best friend, Jennifer Lee, in amazement. "The boys' cross-country team, Jennifer; remember who their star runner is?"

"Eric Powers," Jennifer said. "So what? He must have seen you working out hundreds of times."

Kelly tossed down her brush in disgust. "Have you ever tried to do thirty sit-ups after running three miles? I could barely do ten. But what was really humiliating," she added, "is that Coach

Hayes made Eric hold my ankles while I did them."

Jennifer finally understood her friend's embarrassment. "Not Eric."

Kelly nodded. "There I was, tired and sweaty, with the coach barking at me and Eric holding onto my feet."

Unsuccessfully, Jennifer tried to smother a giggle. "You always wanted Eric at your feet," she managed to say before bursting into helpless laughter.

"You're not very original," Kelly snorted, tossing her thick curly brown hair over her shoulder as she bent to tie her sneakers. "Everyone on the team made that same joke. It was awful."

"That does sound awful," Jennifer agreed, wiping her eyes. "What did Eric do?"

Kelly bit her lower lip, trying not to look too proud of herself. "He laughed with everyone else at first, but when I finally collapsed he helped me up and said I could be on his team anytime. He called me a real trouper."

"How romantic," Jennifer said wryly.

"It was," Kelly insisted. "You should have seen his eyes when he said it; they were so serious, and deep, deep blue, and he looked so cute in his track suit . . ."

"And then?"

"'And then' what?" Kelly said, lost in her memory of Eric's rare words of praise.

"Did he ask you out?"

"He was too busy with practice," Kelly said. She finished dressing with only a casual glance in the mirror.

This was one Saturday that Kelly didn't have to worry about her looks; an afternoon catching up on homework with Jennifer lay ahead of her. Sometimes Kelly really wondered about herself; here she was, with a brand new career as a professional model, and yet she was relieved to have a day off, without anyone to criticize her hair and makeup. Sometimes she wondered if she was really cut out to be a model after all.

Jennifer idly picked up Kelly's hairbrush, but not to use it. Her own dark, glossy hair never seemed to be out of place. Everything about Jennifer was neat and well organized; her clothes, her study habits—even her advice.

"Eric will come around," she told Kelly. "He's too shy for his own good when it comes to girls, but I know he likes you."

"He's shy when it comes to me, you mean; but thanks." Kelly stretched carefully and grimaced as a sore muscle twitched, reminding her of those extra sit-ups.

"It's lucky that with cross-country practice, you see so much of him," Jennifer pointed out. "Just living across the street from him isn't enough; you have to get him so used to seeing Kelly Blake that he starts to miss you when you're not around. Practice is perfect for that—while it lasts. Soon you'll be so busy modeling that you won't have time for running anymore."

"I'll never give up cross-country," Kelly declared hotly. "I love running."

"Running after Eric," Jennifer teased.

Kelly threw three stuffed animals at her, which Jennifer promptly threw back; they were laughing so hard they barely heard the phone ringing.

"It's Eric," Jennifer shrieked. "It's Eric calling his dreamgirl for a date—he wants to run around the block with you!"

Kelly motioned sharply for Jennifer to be quiet. "It's FLASH!," she whispered, holding one hand over the mouthpiece, and Jennifer sobered instantly. They never called on Saturday—something special must be up.

FLASH! was the hottest modeling agency in New York City, and Jennifer knew Kelly was incredibly lucky to be working for them. In fact, it was Jennifer who had convinced Kelly to go to the beauty make-overs where she had been discovered by Meg Dorian, the head of FLASH!. Almost overnight, Kelly had become Meg's most promising new model.

Yet Kelly was frowning when she hung up the phone. "I got my next assignment," she said glumly.

"What's wrong? You don't look very excited."

"That was Nina, my booker—the woman who keeps track of all my appointments," she explained. "She says I have to do a runway show. Live modeling at some fancy charity ball, a benefit for the Children's Fund."

Jennifer was confused. "What does FLASH! have to do with a charity benefit?"

"Nina said something about publicity. I don't know. There's going to be a fashion show before a big dinner dance, and I have to go as a representative from FLASH!."

"Maybe it's an honor to be chosen."

Kelly shook her head doubtfully. "It sounds like punishment to me. I don't know anything about runway modeling; I've never been in a fashion show in my life."

"Yes, you have; we both were," Jennifer said, "and you were the star of the show."

"Jennifer, be serious," Kelly said. "That was in

sixth grade, for our Girl Scout troop, and I was the 'star' because I fell flat on my face and everybody laughed."

"We both fell—Nancy Nathanson tripped and we fell over her, remember?" Jennifer giggled. "But you wouldn't fall now—you're a professional model."

"I don't believe you're saying this, Jen. Don't you understand? I can't get up on a runway wearing high heels in front of two hundred famous people; I can barely walk in high heels! Why did I ever let you talk me into this thing?"

Grabbing the phone, Kelly began to dial the FLASH! agency, but Jennifer pressed down on the base, breaking the connection.

"Let go, Jen," Kelly cried. "I'm calling them back—I'll tell her I can't do it."

"You're really afraid of this show, aren't you?"

"Of course I am." She collapsed onto the bed. "It's all so new to me. I never really believed I was model material, anyway; the only people who ever thought I was pretty were you and my mother. Then Meg Dorian discovered me, and suddenly I have to think of myself in a whole new way. Jennifer," she said, grabbing her friend's shoulders and forcing her to look straight into her face, "do I really look like a high-fashion model to you? Be objective."

"Of course you do," Jennifer stated emphatically. Kelly was the perfect model as far as she was concerned; tall and healthy-looking, with a face that could be simply pretty or downright beautiful; curly brown hair that showed golden highlights in the sun; and those blue-green eyes—clear and honest.

"Models today are all individuals, Kelly, not

cookie-cutter pretty—and that's what you are, a real individual."

Kelly jumped up and went to the mirror in disgust. "I'll say I am! My hair is completely unmanageable and my mouth is much too wide. I'm not in the least delicate, and I'm not exotic-looking, either. Honestly, Jen, I think I'm pretty ordinary."

"I don't think so and Meg Dorian doesn't think so," Jennifer stated flatly, "and most important, the camera doesn't think so."

"Exactly!" Kelly said. "The camera."

It was true; to Kelly's surprise, the pictures from her first photo session had been knockouts. But that was after a makeup artist and hairdresser had worked on her, as well as a top-notch photographer.

"I look great in photographs, but there is no camera at a live fashion show. It's going to be the real me up there, where everyone can see me. Sure, I'll have my hair done and makeup on, but it will be me walking down that runway, and I bet I'll fall flat on my face, just like I did in sixth grade."

"You're crazy," Jennifer said. "What about the track team?"

Kelly was baffled. "So?"

"You're an athlete now—a good one from what Coach Hayes says. Don't you think an athlete like you can handle a little stroll down a runway?"

Kelly hadn't thought of it that way; since joining the track team she had developed her coordination, and her muscle tone was superb. But that had nothing to do with parading in front of hundreds of important people—she could still make a fool of herself. Jennifer, however, had that no-nonsense look on her face and Kelly knew better than to argue. Jennifer's logical mind suited her interest in science, but Jennifer sometimes forgot people's feelings aren't logical.

"Maybe I can handle the runway," Kelly said slowly, "but there's another thing that bothers me. I hate to sound selfish, but I'm not sure I'm interested in this benefit thing. If I'm going to be a model, I want to be a *top* model, and that means magazine covers. I want to be a cover girl. No one cares about runway models. They're not famous, nobody knows their names."

"That's true," Jennifer agreed. "I've never heard of a runway model making it big."

"And I have to make it big, Jen." Kelly studied a framed photograph on her dresser: it showed her with her mother, her half sister, Tina, and her stepfather, Hal Blake. Sitting on the steps of a cabin in the mountains, their arms around each others' shoulders, it seemed the picture of a happy, ordinary family. Yet her family wasn't exactly ordinary.

Years ago, Kelly's mother, Judith, had married impulsively and foolishly. Kelly's real father, from whom she'd inherited her height, her dark hair, and her athletic build, lived in California now. Despite their physical similarities, the two weren't close. Kelly hadn't seen him in ten years. For as long as she could remember, Hal Blake had been her father.

A police officer in Franklyn, Hal was the kind of steady, loyal family man who stopped to help lost kids or rescue stray cats. He had provided a warm, stable family life for the Blake family, but his salary only paid for the basics. More than anything, Hal and Judith wanted Kelly to go to a good college—and on Hal's salary, that goal was only a dream.

Meg Dorian had appeared like a fairy god-mother, promising bundles of cash and a bright, sky's-the-limit future for Kelly. Kelly knew the salary of a top model could pay for a dozen college educations. If she only did reasonably well, she could easily put herself—and Tina, too—through the state university. If she was the best, she could go anywhere and have everything she or her family ever wanted.

At sixteen, Kelly wasn't sure what she expected to do in life, but easing the worry she had seen on her parents' faces when they spoke of the girls' education wasn't a bad goal—for a start.

"It really is important that I do well as a model, and not just for my own sake," she said slowly.

"I know," Jennifer said, well aware of Kelly's family situation. "I hope I get a scholarship for my own college tuition."

Kelly laughed. "You're one of the smartest kids in school, a scientific genius. You won't have to worry."

"It isn't as easy as it seems, though; I really have to work hard. But anyway, I understand why you need to earn top money modeling."

"Then you agree that this benefit fashion show is a waste of my time?"

Jennifer frowned. "That seems logical, but . . ."

"But what?" Kelly beamed in triumph; Jennifer had agreed with her, and that took some doing. "Admit it, Jen, what I said makes sense. I need all the help I can get doing *real* modeling work. And I intend to say so—Monday afternoon, right after school, I'll go see Meg Dorian in person and tell her how I feel about this charity assignment. I'm sure she'll see things my way. After all, it's my career, and my future, and I should have some say in how it goes."

"I think so," Jennifer agreed. "And Meg Dorian will probably admire you for knowing your own mind."

"That's right." Kelly nodded. "She'll think I'm the kind of person who knows what she wants and goes after it."

"Speaking of which," Jennifer said slyly, "a certain track star just pulled into his driveway across the street."

Kelly leaped to the window, edging Jennifer aside so she could peek through the curtains. Sure enough, Eric's blue Toyota was in the driveway of the white shingled house across the street, and Eric's long legs, still clad in sweatpants, swung out of the driver's seat. Eric appeared, all six-foot-one of him, and Kelly let the curtains drop into place so he wouldn't catch her spying on him.

"The poor guy," Jennifer said mournfully. "Not a moment's privacy. Do you think his family would have moved here this summer if anyone had told them they'd be living across the street from a genuine Peeping Tom?"

Kelly left the window entirely. "I don't have to spy on Eric—I have better things to do."

"Like what?" Jennifer grinned.

"English lit, bio, and French." She grabbed her school books and headed for the stairs. "Come on, Jennifer," she called airily, "there's more to life than boys."

Two

Coming into the city alone still gave Kelly a thrill. Two years ago, the city was someplace she went only with her parents. A year ago it became someplace she went to see a play or to attend a concert. And when she first started to model, her mother usually drove her in. Now she'd started taking the bus in and out of the city on her own. Yet she still felt a twinge of excitement when the city's impressive skyline showed through the bus window.

"Is Meg in?" she asked the FLASH! receptionist, trying to give an impression of confidence. "I just need to see her for one minute."

The receptionist, busy with a dozen ringing phone lines, waved her toward Meg's office. "See for yourself," she snapped, covering the receiver with one hand.

Kelly knew Meg had an open-door policy with her models, but the busy FLASH! offices made Kelly feel polite and strained. She regretted her decision to face Meg in person; a phone call might have been better after all.

"Are you going in or are you lost?" the receptionist asked, and everyone in the waiting room looked at Kelly curiously. The lobby, as always, was crowded; models and aspiring models lined the couches, some killing time until their bookings, some with no assignments scheduled but lingering in the offices "just in case"—in case one of the busier, more popular models came down with the flu, or quit in a fit of bad temper, or eloped with a new boyfriend—anything that got them the job.

"I'm going right in."

Kelly allowed herself a small feeling of superiority; never, she vowed, would she be reduced to begging for work. She planned to be available and cooperative at all times and make herself one of the most sought-after models the FLASH! agency had ever seen. *Except for this one benefit job, that is,* she thought.

Kelly summoned up her courage and plunged down the long hall that led to Meg Dorian's private office. Beautiful girls were everywhere. Phones rang incessantly; subdued panic filled the air—Kelly suddenly felt small and unimportant. But she had come this far, and she had to stick to her decision. She reminded herself of what Jennifer had said: Meg would respect Kelly for knowing her own mind.

The door to Meg's office stood open, but Kelly knocked politely before entering. Meg had company: a striking girl with flaming red hair was bent over Meg's desk, speaking in urgent tones. The talk stopped instantly as Kelly appeared at the door.

"Kelly," Meg said, surprise showing in her handsome strong-boned face, "I didn't expect to see you today. Do you have a booking?"

Kelly hesitated—the red-haired girl was clearly annoyed at the interruption and Kelly regretted her bad timing. Yet Meg motioned her calmly into the office.

"I'm glad you stopped by. Kelly, this is Paisley Gregg, one of my best girls. Paisley, meet Kelly Blake—my latest find."

Paisley ignored the hand Kelly held out to her, narrowed her dark eyes, and openly examined Kelly from head to toe. Without flinching, Kelly stared back.

Paisley's name suited her perfectly: everything about her was unusually dramatic, almost theatrical, from her severely cropped red hair to the near-black eyes flashing against her pale, porcelainlike skin. A spattering of freckles saved her face from an almost too angelic quality. The defiant expression in her eyes showed that Paisley clearly had a temper to match her flaming hair.

With a gesture of dismissal, Paisley tossed a corner of the gay paisley shawl she wore over her shoulder.

"So this is the one you're sending to the Children's Fund benefit." Paisley's slight Southern accent seemed to give a mocking edge to her words. "Not exactly the high-fashion type. You'd be better off sending me, Meg."

Kelly couldn't believe her luck. "That's exactly what I came to talk to you about," she told Meg excitedly. "This fashion show for the Children's Fund—I've been thinking that it's not exactly what I'm interested in. I want to be a cover girl, or at least stick to magazine assignments, and doing this benefit will just be a waste of time for me. Maybe I could switch with Paisley. It would work out perfectly."

Paisley's mouth dropped open; she stared as if Kelly had gone mad in front of her eyes. Meg's eyebrows arched, but she made no other comment on Kelly's speech.

Kelly's nerve weakened. "I—I mean if that's okay with you," she faltered. "It's just that I have so much to learn about photographic work, and I didn't want to get distracted . . ." She ended lamely, not understanding Meg's expressionless face or Paisley's obvious amusement.

"Let me take this *wasteful* assignment off her hands," Paisley drawled in delight. "After all, she has *important* things to do."

Meg spoke quietly. "That's enough, Paisley. Perhaps Kelly doesn't realize the opportunity she's about to pass up."

Paisley hooted loudly. "I'll say she doesn't. Let me have it, Meg; say I can do the show before this *poor soul* realizes what she's done."

Kelly's face flushed red; it was bad enough to realize she had made a terrible blunder, but worse not to know what that blunder was.

"I . . . I'm afraid I don't understand," she stuttered.

"Then let me fill you in." With a deliberateness that Kelly recognized as controlled anger, Meg sat up primly in her leather armchair, folded her hands together, and leaned forward to speak.

"You're new, Kelly—very new, so I'll have to excuse your ignorance."

Meg's voice was impersonal, yet Kelly understood she was being given extra consideration and that another girl might not have been spared the full force of Meg's anger.

"Number one—a special job like this fashion show is a privilege; it is not something to be traded away."

Kelly tried to speak but Meg cut her off.

"Number two—you work for me. I don't mean to sound harsh or unreasonable, Kelly, but let's get this very clear. There are a hundred models in this agency and every one of them wants to make it to the top. I'd be happy if they could all get there—but they can't. Very few have the looks *and* the talent *and* the discipline *and* the ambition to be number one. But the lucky girl who does make it, Kelly, will not make it on her own. She'll have plenty of help on the way. And the most important help, the biggest boost in the right direction, will come from me."

Unable to meet Meg's stern gaze, Kelly turned her eyes aside and caught a glimpse of Paisley struggling to keep a smile off her face. *She's heard this speech before,* Kelly realized with a shock, and instantly she felt a wave of relief. There was no mistaking the seriousness of Meg's message, but she was glad to know she wasn't the only one of Meg's models who had ever made the mistake of doubting Meg's judgment.

"I take all this quite seriously, Kelly," Meg continued. "I don't trifle with any girl's career. Each assignment is an opportunity—a stepping stone—to go on to a better assignment. To become better known, to earn the respect of others in the business. Now," Meg paused, taking a deep breath, "now we come to the Children's Fund show. Paisley—maybe you can explain why Kelly might want to do this benefit."

"Are you kidding?" Paisley flung her arms open wide. "Exposure—the best exposure in the business. How old are you, honey?"

"Sixteen," Kelly answered resentfully. She was getting the idea, and it hardly seemed necessary for this Paisley person to act so superior. Kelly was no dummy; she never made the same mistake twice.

Paisley went on in the same smug tone of voice, obviously relishing the chance to show Kelly how stupidly she had acted.

"Sixteen—a total beginner, and in one night you'll have a chance to be seen by the most important people in the business—all of them in one room. Do you have any idea who attends this society bash?" Paisley counted on her fingertips. "Every top designer, every beauty executive, every editor from every important paper and magazine in the country, every top agent and talent scout . . . I could go on and on!"

Kelly didn't doubt that; Paisley showed no signs of stopping. Kelly shifted from foot to foot, wishing she had the nerve to sit down in one of the comfortable chairs flanking Meg's desk.

"In one night, more powerful people will see you than in a year's worth of interviews and go-sees. It's every model's *dream.* You could land a million-dollar exclusive contract because of a show like this—Clyde Mason himself could ask you to be his exclusive model! He could design his next line of clothes for *you*; your look could be the image every woman in America wants to copy. Every woman in the *world!*"

"Thank you, Paisley." With a smile, Meg

waved the girl to a stop. "I think Kelly gets the idea."

"I certainly do," Kelly said meekly. "I should have realized, Meg. I'm sorry"—she glanced at Paisley resentfully, wishing the girl would leave the room so at least she could apologize in private—"I'm sorry I was ungrateful."

"All right; enough apologies," Meg said briskly. "Back to business."

With a frown, Paisley gathered her things together.

"Just a minute, Paisley." Meg crossed her arms thoughtfully. "As it happens, I'm able to send more than one girl from FLASH! to the benefit. And obviously, Kelly needs to be shown the ropes."

The change was remarkable; instantly, Paisley dropped her sophisticated manner. Hopping behind the desk, she hugged Meg repeatedly, clapping her hands and practically squealing in delight.

"I have it? For real? Oh, Meg, thank you, thank you, thank you!"

Meg freed herself, a bit breathless from Paisley's enthusiastic hugs. "To be perfectly honest, I intended to send you all along. You made quite a hit with Clyde Mason last year. His assistant called and requested you do this year's show too."

Paisley's expression became reverent. "Clyde Mason asked for *me*?" She clung to the edge of Meg's desk as though she might fall over. Clyde Mason, as Kelly well knew, was one of the brightest new designers on the fashion scene.

Meg watched Paisley with amusement. "Save the acting for your drama coach," she said dryly.

"Will I model for Clyde Mason also?" Kelly

asked. An image flashed in her mind: Clyde's latest ad campaign featured a double-page spread of spacy-looking models with spray-painted hair and faces. She could hardly picture herself as one of them.

"You will," Meg replied. "I think your look and Clyde's clothes are a happy combination."

"Her?" Paisley didn't bother to conceal her disbelief. "With that hair?"

Before Kelly could defend herself, Meg had moved to the door, ushering Paisley outside. "You'd better hurry to that booking," she said, closing the door firmly behind Paisley.

Kelly had mixed feelings. Meg had gotten her excited about the benefit, but she could hardly picture herself as a Clyde Mason model.

"Take that worried look off your face," Meg said, laughing. "You shouldn't mind Paisley; she has a way of saying exactly what she thinks, but she isn't always right."

"But she is sometimes," Kelly guessed.

"You can learn from Paisley; she's ambitious, and tough, and determined." Abruptly, Meg's manner became businesslike again. "Enough about Paisley Gregg. There's another reason my girls do the Children's Fund benefit each year. Have you ever heard of Herbert Von Metzenberg?"

Kelly shook her head no, thinking that Paisley Gregg, undoubtedly, would know exactly who and what Herbert Von Metzenberg was.

"Just think of him as Santa Claus." Meg smiled. "He's quite rich and quite powerful, and very generous. In fact, he's the sponsor of the Children's Fund benefit; if it weren't for him, the charity would lose most of its largest contributors. He's also an old and very dear friend of mine."

Kelly smiled. "He sounds very nice."

"I also find," Meg added, "that being a friend of Herbert's doesn't hurt business. If you meet him at the benefit, and you probably will, try to remember that. Be polite, Kelly."

Kelly was mystified by Meg's subtle warning. *Why wouldn't I be polite to anyone I met, and especially this Von Metzenberg, if he's a good friend of Meg's?*

Before she could reply, Meg had turned her thoughts elsewhere. "As long as you're here, Kelly, let's see if we can send you out on some calls."

"But I'm not prepared," Kelly protested. "It's so late in the day—I didn't bring anything with me." Lately, Kelly had taken to carrying her model's kit—a big black bag stuffed with makeup and curling rods—to school with her in case of sudden emergencies, like the time she replaced another model at the last minute.

The bag really came in handy, but since Mondays were usually booked by the previous Friday afternoon, Kelly had felt safe in leaving it behind today. There didn't seem to be much chance of a last-minute booking.

"Go see Nina," Meg commanded. "She may have something for you."

Obediently, Kelly headed for the door.

"Wait a minute—is that a limp? Is that ankle still bothering you?" Meg stared. "That's the foot you hurt running, isn't it?"

"It's nothing," Kelly said, touched by Meg's concern. "It hardly bothers me at all anymore . . ."

"Be more careful," Meg said briskly. "We can't have you hobbling around on assignment, you'll throw off the line of the clothes."

Some sympathy! Meg cared more about clothes than Kelly's pain! But Kelly caught herself; she was a model now, and everything about her body was Meg's business. She held back an impulse to answer, "Yes, sir!" in the snappy way Coach Hayes had trained the track team to answer him.

Instead she managed to say, "Yes, I will." Then she wrenched open the office door and burst into the hall, laughing with relief. Imagine what Meg would say—being compared to Kelly's cross-country coach! *Though they certainly are a lot alike*, Kelly thought.

Of course, Coach Hayes was as stout and sloppy as Meg Dorian was trim and well groomed. Coach couldn't be bothered with unimportant, time-consuming chores like getting a haircut regularly or ironing, whereas Meg Dorian, the picture of the successful executive woman, never had a strand of her graying dark hair out of place. Her makeup was flawless over the strong, high cheekbones that gave her an air of power and authority, and only the best, perfectly maintained fabrics clothed her imposing, tall frame.

But there the differences ended. Coach Hayes accepted no excuses for laziness or lack of dedication, was ruthless when punishment was deserved, and demanded absolute discipline. Meg Dorian, Kelly suspected, was even tougher.

Nina, Kelly's booker, had no last-minute calls for Kelly to make, which was fine with Kelly. She was glad to see a few empty spaces on the "Hollywood" board where her name, along with those of Meg's other top girls, was listed next to spaces for the hours of the day. From the look of things, she had a busy week coming up, and every spare moment was a moment to be savored.

"Everything okay?" The receptionist eyed her curiously as Kelly headed toward the door.

"Super," Kelly replied for the benefit of the girls still waiting in the lobby. "Just straightening out details for the Children's Fund ball!" Waving gaily, she made a grand exit.

Once on the bus back to New Jersey, she could giggle at the scene; all those faces, admiring and envying the confident model—if only they knew how nervous Kelly had been, and how close she had come to ruining her chances with Meg! She was relieved that the afternoon's dreaded confrontation had ended well.

Idly, Kelly leafed through the fashion magazines she had bought in the bus station to read on the way home.

Hey, I know this girl, she thought, staring at a full-page spread. Automatically, she went through her classes at Franklyn High, trying to place the familiar face: was she in her English lit class? geometry? biology? French? With a start, Kelly sat up in her seat, and the stack of magazines slid from her lap to the floor. Franklyn High—what was she thinking of? The girl was Paisley Gregg! Paisley's pixie face, disguised under glamorous evening makeup, stared at her from the pages of *Couture* magazine—someone she had talked to that very afternoon!

Kelly quickly picked up the rest of the magazines and flipped through the pages with mounting excitement. Why, already she recognized many of these models—some were girls from FLASH!, or girls she had seen in halls and elevators on her way to an assignment.

Her eyes dancing, Kelly leaned back in her seat as the New York skyline receded in the distance. She felt strangely unreal: she knew the faces in the magazines that thousands—millions —of people read, all over the country, all around the world. And she was one of them—a professional model.

Three

As usual the halls of Franklyn High were crowded, especially near the lockers. Kelly had to push her way forward.

"Kelly—over here," Jennifer called gaily, spotting Kelly's dark head.

"Hi, Rochelle, hi, Lisa." Kelly inched her way past the junior girls grouped around Jennifer. "I can think of better ways to start the day than being crushed to death every morning. Wouldn't it be nice to have some real space—a locker room for every three students."

"You don't have to worry about getting lost in a crowd, big shot," Lisa Daly teased.

"What are you talking about?" Kelly looked quizzically at Lisa.

"I guess you haven't seen the morning paper," Jennifer said. She grabbed the newspaper from Lisa. "*This* is a great way to start the day." While

Lisa and Rochelle Sherman and several other girls crowded around, Jennifer read out loud:

"'This year's Children's Fund Benefit Ball promises to be more star-studded than ever before. Celebrities by the dozen are snapping up the five-hundred-dollar-a-plate-dinner tickets, the hottest invitation in town since millionaire Herbert Von Metzenberg became the ball's honorary chairman five years ago. Von Metzenberg promises an astronomical donation to the Fund from this year's ball, and stars from Hollywood to Broadway seem anxious to help him keep his promise.'

"Then there are pictures of movie and television stars buying tickets," Jennifer explained, showing the paper to Kelly.

"I guess I'm glad Meg talked me into doing the fashion show," Kelly said.

"You guess?" Lisa rolled her eyes. "I'd give anything to be in your shoes."

"Promise you'll touch Robert Redford for me," Rochelle cooed.

"Never mind the movie stars," Lisa cut in, "look at the rock stars that are going! This is some bash, Kelly. Are you really going to be there?"

"In the flesh," Kelly quipped easily. It was fun to talk about her modeling career with Lisa and Rochelle. With Jennifer, they were among her few friends who didn't seem to feel that modeling had changed her overnight.

Behind them, Bobbi Simmons and Lynn Graves, standing in the crush of bodies, turned to glare.

"Excuse me," Bobbi said in an exaggerated drawl. "The air here is a little rich for my blood."

Purposely turning their backs, the two brushed past Kelly, noses in the air.

Kelly's cheeks reddened as she stared at their retreating backs.

"Forget them," Lisa advised. "They're not worth worrying about."

"But I hate it when people treat me that way!" Kelly said. "I never said I was better than them—why can't they just act normal around me? I never rub it in that I'm a model—sometimes I don't even believe it myself!"

"Forget it," Jennifer urged. "You don't have to be a model to be better than those two! So what if they think you're a snob. The way they act, they're bigger snobs than you ever were! And everyone knows it, too."

"But I hate it when people avoid me," Kelly said.

"I like them better than the other types," Jennifer answered.

"What other types?" Lisa and Rochelle crowded closer.

"You know—the types who try to butter me up." Kelly grinned.

"That's right," Jennifer said, "like our beloved head cheerleaders, who never gave me or Kelly the time of day. Suddenly they're Kelly's best friends."

"They are not," Kelly corrected her. "Thank goodness I have you, and Rochelle and Lisa, too—real friends who like me for what I am."

"What you are," Rochelle sighed, "is a model invited to this fabulous ball. I would kill to get there. But then, I probably wouldn't have a thing to say to someone famous, even if I did go. And I'd have to spend two years of my allowance on something to wear. And I'd have to give up eating for at least six months beforehand."

Kelly handed the newspaper back to Jennifer. "I didn't realize so many stars were going—I thought it was mainly fashion people. You know, people connected to modeling and magazines. And society, of course—but I don't know a thing about high society."

"Keep your eyes open, Kelly," Lisa advised. "There may be a young, handsome, filthy rich society boy there who's dying to go out with a normal high-school girl like me."

"Sure," Jennifer teased, "some guy who's tired of the jet set and longs for a quiet evening in New Jersey."

"What's this about the jet set?"

All heads turned as Eric Powers, whose locker was nearby, joined their crowd. Kelly flushed. Eric was the last person to be impressed by society or movie stars, and Kelly prayed the girls wouldn't make a fuss over the newspaper item in front of him.

"I was kidding," Jennifer explained. "We were talking about this big charity bash Kelly's going to." She showed Eric the newspaper article.

"I'm not going to it," Kelly corrected. "I'm going to be working at it, doing a fashion show."

Eric whistled at the long list of celebrities' names. "Sounds more like the Academy Awards than a charity ball. Impressive."

"Celebrities are just human beings," Kelly tried to say casually; but somehow the comment came out all wrong—it sounded as if she were bragging, and that would never do, not as far as Eric was concerned.

"What I mean is," she added hastily, "you

shouldn't be impressed by a bunch of movie stars. They're just people doing their jobs, only their jobs happen to be glamorous."

"Like modeling," Rochelle said. Kelly could have killed her for making things worse.

"Listen, Eric," Lisa said flippantly. "Kelly promised to bring home a movie star for each of us. Better put your order in—which of these glamorous ladies would you like?" She took the paper from Jennifer and held it out to Eric.

Playing along, he squinted his eyes appraisingly, then let out a long, mournful sigh. "None of them look like computer experts," he said, "and if I don't get help fast, I'm going to flunk my advanced programming exam."

"Isn't that class the worst," Jennifer groaned. Since the advanced computer course was an elective, both Jennifer—a junior, like Kelly—and Eric, who was a senior, had been eligible for it. "No one else has a big exam *before* mid-terms."

"They just love to torture us," Eric said, imitating a mad scientist.

"Uggh," Lisa and Rochelle grimaced in unison.

"You're disgusting, Eric," Lisa said, as she and Rochelle headed for their homerooms.

Eric pretended to stalk after them but soon turned back to Jennifer, laughing. "Seriously, Jennifer, how are you doing in programming?" he asked.

Kelly watched jealously as Jennifer and Eric discussed their latest computer project. She wished Eric had teased *her* instead of Lisa and Rochelle.

"Oh, no!" she cried suddenly. Eric and Jennifer looked at her curiously and she blushed even deeper. "I was supposed to meet my lab partner after school yesterday, to do over that dissection project we botched in class, and I totally forgot."

"If Alfred Lindel was my lab partner, I'd have forgotten it, too," Jennifer said loyally.

Alfred was one of those boys who never quite fit in. Pudgy and slow-minded, he was never included in any of the groups at school, though Kelly and Jennifer were as friendly to him as they would be to anyone they had known since first grade.

"You probably have to work twice as hard to cover Lindel's mistakes," Eric said sympathetically.

"You're not kidding." Kelly frowned; now she had to make up the project today, and she'd be late for cross-country practice, which meant both her bio teacher, Mr. Cranston, and Coach Hayes would be angry with her. "This modeling business can be a real pain," she muttered.

Eric looked at her in surprise. "I never thought I'd hear you say anything bad about modeling. I thought it was the greatest thing since sliced bread."

Kelly's temper flared. "Look—I'm proud of my modeling," she said quickly. "Why shouldn't I be? Models aren't dumb, they aren't fluffheads . . ."

Eric's smile faded. "I didn't mean . . ."

"Modeling is a real profession," she declared hotly, "like any other, and, and . . ." She began to stutter, her cheeks really flaming now. Eric looked totally uncomfortable, but she couldn't seem to stop.

". . . models work hard . . . They put themselves through college modeling, and they become doctors and lawyers and—and anything they want!" Her voice had become louder and other people stopped to stare. Mortified by her outburst, Kelly wheeled toward her homeroom, her heart pounding furiously. She felt completely ridiculous for creating a scene. And for the worst reason! She'd felt defensive over the way modeling was cutting into her time, so she took it out on Eric.

Suddenly an arm reached out, blocking her way. *Eric!* Kelly thought—but the hope faded quickly when she glanced up to find Cliff Sturgess, all one hundred seventy muscle-bound pounds of him, looming over her.

"I hear you're a big-league model now," Cliff said. His hair was only inches away from hers— *too close for comfort,* Kelly decided, as the senior football star leaned over her intimately. "Who would have thought skinny little Kelly Blake would grow into . . ."

"Into what?" Kelly demanded. She didn't share Cliff's opinion that he was Franklyn High's most desirable male, and she was in no mood for any more conversations with irritating boys.

"Into centerfold material." Cliff leered at her, and Kelly pushed against his arm to get by, but Cliff was too strong to be budged. He leaned even closer, his outstretched arms pinning her against the row of lockers. She could feel a combination lock poking into her back.

"You heard wrong," Kelly said. "I'm no centerfold."

"Oh, yeah?" Cliff took a long, frank look at Kelly's body. "I'll have to see for myself before I make up my mind."

"Some other time," Kelly said calmly, although she felt anything but calm. Cliff was used to a pretty fast crowd; too fast for her tastes.

"When?" Cliff leaned even closer. "Like tonight, maybe?"

"Like never," Kelly said. "I'm not interested, okay?"

Cliff laughed, his breath puffing into her face. "You're cute, you know that? I never thought you were the model type. I mean, you were always tall, but scrawny. And the way you hang out with that Jennifer Lee, Miss Brain of New Jersey . . . I thought models were more glamorous."

Kelly was beginning to feel a little desperate. Since direct rejection had no effect on Cliff, maybe she could use flattery to get rid of him.

"I really appreciate your asking me out, Cliff," she said, trying to sound as if she meant it, "but I wouldn't want anyone to get the wrong idea. After all, you're a pretty popular guy and you already have a girlfriend, don't you? I wouldn't want to be seen with you; it might mess up your social life."

Cliff grinned. "Who's talking about my social life? I just thought you and me could get to know each other, kind of make up for lost time, if you know what I mean."

Kelly gave up. "I've got to go," she said. "There's the bell."

"Not till you say it's a date."

The halls were emptying fast. She searched for someone to help her out, but Jennifer and her other friends had already gone to homeroom, and Kelly couldn't ask a total stranger to rescue her.

Cliff reached for the stack of notebooks she cradled in her arms. "Come on, I'll walk you to class and we'll discuss tonight."

"Cliff, no! I don't want to," she said, trying to grab her books away from him. Her words sounded lame, even to herself—she sounded like a baby, or worse, as if she was playing along with him, flirting or playing hard to get.

Cliff must have thought so, too; he laughed and kept laughing, walking backward down the hall, the two of them struggling over her notebooks. She was almost glad no one was around; she'd die of embarrassment if anyone saw her now.

"Cliff, I'll really be late, come on . . ."

He was leading her toward the swinging doors in front of the stairway. The far stairwell was a notorious make-out spot for some of Franklyn High's couples. Kelly had never been there with any boy, and she certainly didn't want to be there with a boy like Cliff.

She was scared, and angry with herself for being scared. *I should be able to take care of myself better than this*, she thought.

"I know what you model types are like," Cliff was saying. "The wild parties you go to . . ."

She was on the verge of dropping her books and running when, suddenly, someone put his arm around her from behind.

She froze, too confused to think calmly, when Eric's voice, firm and calm, sounded in her ear.

"Weren't you supposed to meet me here, Kelly?"

Cliff finally let go of her notebooks, and Kelly tried not to breathe too big a sigh of relief. "Was I?" she gulped, steadying her frazzled nerves.

Eric draped his arm casually around her shoulders. "Sure you were. Just like every morning."

Cliff was backing away. "Hey, sorry, Powers—I didn't know she was your property."

"Tough luck." Eric shrugged, grinning at Cliff. Kelly almost expected them to wink at each other; Eric and Cliff acted as though they shared an enormous joke. She didn't enjoy having Cliff think she was anybody's property, and she didn't like the knowing look he gave Eric, either. But Cliff was gone, and she was grateful.

"Thanks," she said, suddenly aware of the weight of Eric's arm around her shoulders.

"He *was* bothering you, wasn't he?" Eric was suddenly anxious. "I mean, you don't like that guy, or anything?"

Kelly groaned. "Cliff Sturgess is not my idea of Prince Charming." Eric *was*, though—did he realize that?

"Sorry for telling him that I meet you here every morning," Eric said, taking his arm away.

"That's okay; you had to tell him something." Kelly felt a sense of loss. What would it be like to really meet Eric every day in the stairwell before classes, to stand with his arm around her, the way they had been a minute ago—Eric's girl for real?

"He backed off fast enough," she said, starting to giggle. "I think Cliff Sturgess was a little afraid of you."

"He was." Eric grinned. "I might have hesitated if I'd thought about it, but I . . ."

"You what?" Kelly gazed at him hopefully. Had he guessed the way she truly felt about him? It must show. Jennifer had known, even before Kelly confessed that she couldn't get Eric out of her mind. *If only this once*, Kelly wished, *I could say what I really mean to say; if only I wouldn't get tongue-tied or flustered.*

Eric finished his sentence. "I didn't think about it because anybody would rescue a nice girl from Cliff. Anyway, next time you get in trouble, choose someone smaller—Sturgess is pretty big."

"You're athletic, too," she protested. "You're strong."

Eric laughed and backed away, a shy look coming into his eyes. Kelly panicked; just when they were finally talking about personal things, Eric looked as if he were going to run away.

"Anyway, I'm not anyone's property," she blurted. "I hate that—I hate the way he talks about girls."

"Sturgess doesn't know much about girls like you," Eric agreed. He hesitated. "Look, Kelly—I owe you an apology. That's why I was looking for you. I never thought of you as a fluffhead, and I know you work hard at running and at modeling, too."

"That's okay," she said quickly. "I overreacted before. I was just feeling pressured, I guess, with so much to do—I don't know how I'll ever get everything done. Especially biology."

"Well, you'd better get those pretty green eyes into a science book," he teased, "or you'll be one top model that flunked biology."

He gave a little wave before hurrying down the hall to his homeroom. Kelly knew she had to get to her own class, but she stood rooted to the spot. She felt a stab of hope; maybe Eric was really thinking seriously about her.

She hurried to homeroom; she was much too late to slip in unnoticed, and Mrs. Belvedere was one of those teachers who thought the dreary morning announcements were sacred—she handed out detention to latecomers at the drop of a hat.

Naturally, everyone stared when Kelly entered

the room as noiselessly as possible and took her seat. Mrs. Belvedere glared at her, but made no comment because the principal's voice was droning endlessly over the P.A. system.

"What happened to you?" Jennifer whispered. "You disappeared."

"With Cliff Sturgess, no thanks to you," Kelly hissed. "Where were you when I needed you?"

Jennifer stared at her, bewildered. "Walking to homeroom."

"It's okay," Kelly said quickly. "Eric found me and rescued me from Cliff."

Jennifer's mouth dropped open in surprise. "Huh?" she said. But suddenly Mrs. Belvedere was in front of them, and Kelly realized the room was totally quiet. Announcements had ended. A quick look around convinced her that most of the homeroom had overheard her whispered conversation with Jennifer.

"Kelly," Mrs. Belvedere rasped, "not only were you very late this morning, but you're very rude besides. The rest of the class was trying to hear the announcements, but all we heard was you."

Cheeks burning, Kelly ignored the jeers and giggles of her classmates as she watched Mrs. Belvedere take out the pad she reserved for writing detention slips. *Great*, she thought. *All I need is detention, when I already have cross-country practice and biology lab to make up.*

Jennifer gave her a quick look of sympathy. "Sorry," she mouthed silently.

Kelly tucked her detention slip into her notebook with a sigh. So much for bio lab and track practice; detention canceled out anything else. She wasn't the type to get detention often, and she dreaded the comments and sneers she'd have to endure from the regulars in detention hall that afternoon.

"All right, class," Mrs. Belvedere announced in her raspy voice. "You may talk quietly among yourselves for the remainder of the period." Thirty voices began chattering at once.

"Now tell me," Jennifer demanded, swiveling to face Kelly. "What in the world happened?"

Kelly embellished every detail of her encounter with Cliff that morning; by the time she finished, the episode sounded like the plot for a torrid romance novel, with Cliff Sturgess the evil villain and Eric the gallant hero, arriving in the nick of time to save Kelly from a fate worse than death.

"Well, I don't get it," Jennifer said as Kelly ended her story. "Eric rescues you and then he just disappears. Didn't he ask you out, or anything?"

"Come on, Jen, give the guy a break. He got rid of Sturgess for coming on too strong to me; he couldn't come on to me himself."

"He could have asked you out. Does he like you or not?" Jennifer persisted. "I don't understand that boy at all, and you must be going crazy."

"I am," Kelly admitted. They'd had a few friendly dates, but she had no idea whether Eric saw the kind of future in their relationship that she did.

"He's just slow," Jennifer said loyally. "It takes boys like Eric a long time to get serious about a girl."

But that wasn't really good news. Kelly knew of several other girls Eric had dated casually since moving to Franklyn that summer, and she didn't want to give anyone else the chance to move in on him while he was making up his mind about her.

"Personally, I think Eric admires you," Jennifer continued. "He's the serious type, and he admires other hard-working types with clear goals."

The bell rang for the first period, and Kelly and Jennifer joined the crowd pushing for the door. *What Jennifer said is true—Eric does admire people with serious goals*, Kelly thought. *But that's exactly what I have—and one goal is to become a top model.* Kelly knew hard work and dedication would go a long way toward achieving that goal. She could see her career progressing in a straight line; all she had to do was take it one step at a time.

But her other goal was more elusive.

"Kelly Blake and Eric Powers," she whispered to herself, as she was pushed toward the door. Kelly and Eric. They sounded perfect together.

Four

"Mom!" Kelly tapped her foot impatiently. She checked her watch again; the rehearsal was in less than an hour, and since Kelly was going to be the only inexperienced model in the fashion show, she wanted to get there in plenty of time.

Leaving her bag filled with makeup, hot rollers, and extra shoes by the front door, Kelly rushed back into the kitchen where her mother was still talking on the phone.

"Mom," Kelly whispered furiously, "I'm going to be late. Come on."

"I'll be right there, Tina," Mrs. Blake was saying hurriedly into the phone. "Calm down."

"Tina?" Kelly said as her mother hung up the phone. "You were talking to Tina?" What did her little sister have to say that was important enough to make her late? "Mom, this fashion show is very important to me. Why didn't you hang up sooner?"

"Kelly, honey, I'll have to drop you at the bus stop on my way to pick up Tina." Her mother glanced at the kitchen clock. "You'll have plenty of time to make the next bus, if we hurry."

Kelly stared. "But you promised me—Mom, you were going to take me right to the hotel. You know I wanted to be early today, and we're going to be late already."

Her mother, buttoning her warm jacket, spoke angrily. "You don't run everything around here, Kelly. Ivy Kallen's mother can't get her car started, and Tina and all her friends are stuck at dancing school with no way to get home. You know what a terrible part of town that is; there's no public transportation and it will be dark soon. Am I supposed to leave Tina stranded?"

"But I'll never make it," Kelly cried. "The bus takes forever, and then I'll have to find a cab and it's Friday afternoon rush hour in the city. Mom, I missed cross-country practice for this!"

"What do you want me to do? I'm not about to pick up Tina and her friends and take them all into the city to drop you and then come back here to drive them all home. Now, please don't argue. I promised Tina I'd get there right away."

It was so unfair. Her mother acted as if Kelly were totally selfish, and that just wasn't true. Mrs. Blake knew how important this rehearsal was to Kelly, and she was nervous enough about it without being late. The agency couldn't care less about Kelly's little sister being stranded at dancing school. *I'll get Tina for this*, Kelly thought.

She stomped out to the car and threw her model's kit into the backseat.

"When's the next bus?" she snapped at her mother.

"Four twenty-seven."

"That's twenty minutes from now! I can't waste that much time, Mom." Calculating quickly, Kelly realized that even if she got a cab instantly, after getting into the city, she would still be at least fifteen minutes late to the rehearsal. "How could you do this to me?"

Cautiously, her mother backed the car down the driveway, keeping an eye out for the toddlers from next door and the assorted pets that had a habit of snoozing under the battered station wagon.

"Really, Kelly, it isn't as if I didn't do the same things for you, when you were Tina's age. You're a big girl now, a working woman, so stop complaining. You couldn't wait to be grown-up and independent—now you are. So act that way."

Kelly endured the rest of the ride in silence; it was useless arguing with her mother where Tina was concerned.

"I'll call from the bus stop when I get home," she said coolly, slamming the car door. "Unless you'd rather I phoned for a cab?"

"Kelly . . . don't be ridiculous. I'll be glad to pick you up later."

Kelly's anger turned to anxiety as she stood in front of the Port Authority Bus Terminal waving wildly at every yellow cab she saw, praying for one to stop. The brilliant afternoon sunshine had faded quickly, and she was painfully aware that her sweater was far too light for the chill air. When a cab finally did stop to pick her up, she jumped in gratefully, only to find that a back window was stuck open. She struggled vainly to close it, angry at the window and with herself.

"Here, keep the change," she yelled, throwing some crunched-up dollar bills at the cab driver and leaping for the curb the minute she saw the Waldorf-Astoria Hotel. At least it would be warm inside, and maybe she could make up some convincing emergency to explain why she was so late. Hugging her heavy bag, she ran past the doorman into the huge lobby, searching for the elevator to the Starlight Roof.

It had sounded so romantic: the Starlight Roof. She had planned a grand entrance, sweeping into the ballroom with studied composure. Instead she was flustered and impatient and shivering. By this time she was a full half hour late!

She flew into the ballroom, barely noticing what it looked like. The room was almost deserted—only five or six people wandered around. Had she gotten it wrong? This near empty room certainly didn't look like the scene of a big rehearsal. Did she dare call Nina this late to double-check? No. It had to be the Waldorf, she couldn't be mistaken about that. Maybe a different ballroom?

Heart sinking, she looked around more carefully. No sign of a runway, no models practicing their dips and turns—it was the wrong day, now she was sure of it. The rehearsal was tomorrow, Saturday, not Friday afternoon. How had she made such a horrendous mistake? If she couldn't even get her assignments straight, maybe it was time to call off her modeling career.

"Kelly Blake, you showed up after all."

Kelly whirled around to find Paisley Gregg, of all people, standing behind her. She sighed in relief; she must have gotten the day right, even if she was now hopelessly late. She could never admit her mistake to Paisley—thinking she came on the wrong day!

"Paisley, where is everyone? I couldn't help being late," she fibbed. "My bus got stuck in traffic and the cab ride took forever!" She sighed in disgust, as if she were used to the perils of commuting back and forth to the city.

Paisley settled herself on a chair at the nearest table and motioned for Kelly to sit.

"I don't know what you expected today, but this is it, honey." She waved at the nearly empty room.

"I don't understand." Kelly narrowed her eyes—was Paisley trying to fool her, take advantage of her inexperience somehow? "Nina said I had to come to this rehearsal, since it was my first live show. Please, Paisley, where and when *is* this rehearsal?"

Paisley laughed out loud. "Honey, this *is* the rehearsal." She seemed to enjoy Kelly's confusion. "Really, I'm not putting you on. Look—see that woman with the clipboard? That's Vanessa, one of Clyde Mason's assistants. She'll double-check your measurements and assign you certain outfits to wear. Vanessa has to coordinate the accessories for each outfit, and after she's had a look at you, she might ask you to bring something she can't supply—which won't be much. One thing about Clyde, he likes to control a model's total look."

Kelly stared at Vanessa, who was indeed taking notes while talking to a girl Kelly now recognized as a model. The girl nodded her head a few times and left.

"But what about the actual rehearsal?" Kelly

insisted. "When do we put on the clothes and walk down the runway, to get the hang of it?"

Paisley stared at her. "I keep forgetting how new you are. For all your instant reputation, you haven't done much, have you, honey?"

"No, *honey*," Kelly replied, losing her patience, "I haven't done much. But I make up for lost time by working very hard, every chance I get."

"Hold on!" Paisley held up her hands in protest. "Don't get on my case. I'm your friend—you don't see anyone else around here running to your rescue, do you?"

Kelly had to admit everyone else in the room was ignoring her. Without Paisley, she would be totally lost. *Still, Paisley doesn't have to act so superior all the time*, she thought. *It's not my fault I'm younger and new to modeling.*

As if reading Kelly's mind, Paisley pointed at the model now leaving the room. "That girl, Mia, was furious when she heard you were doing this show. Lots of girls are jealous of you."

"But I don't even know her," Kelly protested. "She's not with FLASH!—how does she know me?"

"This is a very small world," Paisley told her. "You're Meg Dorian's personal discovery. An average model starting out would have been on a hundred go-sees before getting her first big job, yet you started with a spread in a major magazine." Paisley shook her head pityingly. "You don't realize the breaks you've gotten."

"I'm very grateful to Meg," Kelly said sharply. But to herself, she admitted Paisley's words were a shock. "I know I've had some good assignments," she said, "but it can't be that unusual.

I'm sure Meg helps all her new girls as much as me."

"Ha!" Paisley exclaimed. "Every model in the city envies you." Paisley examined her thoughtfully. "Look, you seem like a genuinely nice kid. I'll introduce you to Vanessa."

Gratefully, Kelly followed Paisley across the ballroom. "I can't believe there's going to be a fashion show here—it's so empty."

"You won't recognize it the night of the benefit," Paisley assured her. "Last year they did an Arabian Nights theme, and everything was totally *smothered* in *miles* of silk. It was *gorgeous!*"

Kelly smiled at Paisley's dramatic manner. There was something basically likable about the older girl, and Kelly admired her self-confidence.

"Paisley"—Kelly hesitated—"how long did it take you to get started? I mean, have you been working for years and years?"

"*Forever,*" Paisley groaned. "Ever since I was sixteen—last year."

It took a minute to sink in. "Sixteen!" Kelly cried, right in front of glamorous Vanessa. "You mean you're only seventeen?" Now she felt like an idiot. Today, and in their earlier encounter, she'd felt—and acted—like an unsophisticated child next to Paisley. *Why did I allow her to intimidate me so much, asking for her advice and hanging onto her every word? Paisley is only a year older than I am!*

Paisley smiled calmly while Kelly stood with her mouth open, looking foolish. Then Paisley introduced her to Vanessa.

"Let's see you with your hair up," Vanessa commanded abruptly as soon as Paisley had completed her introductions.

Kelly held her hair up with one hand, ignoring Paisley's amused glance.

Vanessa pulled out her tape measure. "I have most of your statistics," she explained to Kelly, busily measuring her from head to toe, "but Clyde is very particular. When he designs a dress to cling, he wants it to cling—not billow around a skinny figure. Developed calves," she noted, "perfect for the cropped look. Turn around."

Kelly felt Vanessa lift her sweater and shirt, casually exposing Kelly's back and her flimsy bra to anyone in the room. Kelly held her arms closely across her chest, aware of Paisley's little smirking smile as she did so.

"Aren't we modest," Paisley muttered.

"When I'm older I won't be," Kelly said pointedly. Paisley laughed good-naturedly. *Maybe she isn't so bad after all*, Kelly thought with a flicker of approval. It would be nice to have a friend at the agency.

"Good back," Vanessa noted. "Clyde hates bony spines—they ruin the effect of a backless outfit." Then she put down her clipboard. "Okay, Kelly. You're the last for today. Let's do a quick run-through."

Paisley tagged along as Vanessa guided Kelly to the end of the ballroom.

"The dressing room will be set up in the hallway." She gestured toward the back wall of the ballroom. "You'll enter through that rear door, come out behind the curtains and mount the runway, return, and the dressers will be here, behind the steps. Any questions?"

"Yes," Kelly said. What dressers? how did one mount the runway? how long was it? how long did she stay there? But Vanessa was off and running.

"You'll be perfect," she called, shrugging into a furry mohair sweater-coat. "Don't worry about a thing. We'll see you tomorrow, six or sevenish? Bye-bye."

And she was gone.

Bewildered, Kelly turned to Paisley for help. "I only had about a million questions." She felt like crying. "This just isn't what I expected," she told Paisley, hoping her face didn't show her disappointment.

"You'll catch on." Paisley was busy gathering her things together. "See you tomorrow night."

"Wait," Kelly called frantically. "Paisley, you can't go. I need help. I don't know the first thing about fashion shows. What do I do?"

"You heard Vanessa—just be on time. They'll take care of the rest."

"But I don't know how to do anything." Kelly's voice rose dangerously. Ashamed to let Paisley see how upset she was, she took a deep breath, calming herself. "I guess I'm . . . a little irritated," she finally said. "I missed cross-country practice this afternoon and nearly killed myself to get here. I'm . . . I'm furious that Nina made me come in for *this*." Pretending to be angry helped; the lump in her throat loosened. "Could you just show me how you walk on a runway?"

Sighing, Paisley put down her bags and jacket and shawl and gloves. "Okay. Just once."

Striking a jaunty pose, Paisley bounced toward Kelly, humming a tune out loud. She paused, pivoted two or three times as if showing off a fabulous outfit, then turned sharply and sauntered away from Kelly with an exaggerated, slithering walk.

"But you walked two different ways," Kelly

cried. She imitated Paisley, first bouncing and then slithering. "Which one do I do?"

"I don't know." Paisley shrugged. "I didn't know I had two walks. I just do what comes naturally. If there's music, I listen to that. Sometimes you barely have time to get out there and turn around once before the other girl is out. Other times it takes them forever to read the copy and you're out there like an idiot, striding around with a dopey smile pasted on your face." She shrugged again. "It doesn't really matter what you do."

"But it does matter," Kelly said firmly. "I want Meg to be proud of me. And I want to be proud of myself. Now teach me exactly what to do."

"No one taught *me* to do anything," Paisley explained. "I just imitated the girl in front of me. No one teaches anyone."

"You're going to teach me." Kelly grabbed Paisley's arm. "Just walk me through it once or twice."

They paced up and down, up and down.

"You're kind of a klutz, aren't you?" Paisley said after Kelly had nearly tripped for the third or fourth time.

It was true. Kelly had hoped her running muscles would get her through this ordeal, but she seemed to be doing everything wrong. Instead of being light and natural on her feet, she found herself all stiff and self-conscious. Paisley's slithery walk made her feel indecent, her bouncy stride made her feel clumsy, and she kept bobbing her head every time she took a step forward.

"I'll never get it," she moaned.

"You're just nervous." From the look on Paisley's face, Kelly could tell she didn't believe it herself. The fashion show was sure to be a disaster; why couldn't she just relax and be herself? *I'm an athlete,* Kelly lectured herself sternly, *I can walk up and down a dumb runway in high heels.*

"Just watch me one more time." Kelly stepped away from Paisley, taking a deep breath. Then she took a few steps and pivoted around, her arms swooping after her in a wide, carefree arc. "Free as a bird," she called out, pleased that she had finally gotten it.

"Watch out!" Paisley cried, but it was too late.

Five

Paisley's words of warning echoed in Kelly's ears, but her arms and legs were already wrapped around something cold and hard that threatened to topple down with her to the floor. Then strong arms reached out and caught her.

"Get the camera!" She recognized the voice of Steve Hollender, the photographer who'd shot her first professional layout, and realized that the object she was clinging to was a camera and tripod. But who had his arms around her?

Steve's voice boomed out: "That camera had better be all right!"

Camera? Kelly thought. *What about me?* With her rescuer's help, Kelly caught her balance and straightened up, holding onto the tripod.

"Are you hurt?"

She gazed into the soft gray eyes of the boy who had caught her. Tall, and strong enough to hold both her and the tripod without losing his own balance, he seemed totally in command of the situation. With his arm around her, Kelly suddenly felt self-conscious.

"I'm fine," she said, leaning back to loosen his grip around her waist. Finally he seemed to realize that people were watching, and he stepped back, but without taking his eyes off hers.

"You really ought to watch where you're going, Kelly," Steve Hollender growled. "Remember what happened last time!"

"It wasn't my fault," Kelly defended herself, blushing. "Last time" she had shattered one of Steve's lights into a million pieces. "You shouldn't have sneaked up behind me like that."

"That was my fault," the handsome stranger answered. "I thought I could get a shot of you prancing around—you were off in a dreamworld."

"Enough talk." Steve examined the expensive camera carefully. "You college kids think you know everything. Better not play the big-shot 'artiste' with my equipment, or you won't last long as my assistant."

"You're Steve's assistant?" Kelly looked at the boy in surprise. "I never saw you in the studio. What happened to Bobby, his last assistant?"

"Don't ask." He grinned. "I'm Alex Hawkins."

"Do you want to be a fashion photographer?" she asked.

"I don't know about that yet," he said, laughing. His laugh was charming—casual and spontaneous, the kind of laugh that made you feel good about everything. And Kelly liked the way his curly blond hair, cut well in a fashionably short style, seemed uncombed—as if Alex wasn't vain about his good looks.

Steve looked at Alex irritably. "You don't know yet," he mimicked. "When I was your age I was working steady. You rich kids kill me; think you own the world."

"What's wrong with him?" Kelly asked as Steve moved off to check the lights. "He's usually so friendly."

"He was kind of forced to hire me," Alex admitted. "He owes my father a favor. I guess he's not thrilled with our arrangement, but it's only temporary, for extra college credit. I go to the School of Visual Arts."

"If Steve doesn't like you, shouldn't you find a better job?"

"There are no better jobs," Alex said. "Like it or not, Hollender is about the best in the business. I can learn the most from him."

"Then you *are* serious about photography," Kelly said. For some reason, she hoped Alex wasn't a spoiled rich kid as Steve had implied.

"Always have been. It's just a matter of choosing which kind of photography." Alex frowned. "Some people, like my father, don't think photography is a respectable profession. He wants me to join the family business. But I think people should pursue the things they love, and worry about making money later."

"Sure, I guess so." Kelly wondered what her parents would say about Alex's philosophy. Her mother was thrilled that through modeling, Kelly had a chance to make good money; it would help out the family a lot. And as a policeman, her father had no patience with kids who got into trouble instead of getting into jobs. But Hal Blake also felt his job helped people, and that was more important to him than a big salary.

"Making money doesn't come first with my father, either," she finally decided. "He loves his work."

Alex beamed at her. "You understand me, then. What do you do around here, anyway?"

"She's a model," Steve interrupted. "Kelly, help us out a little, huh?"

"Sure, what do I have to do?"

"Pose. We're meeting a society hotshot here," Steve said gruffly, "to take publicity photos for the Children's Fund benefit. Let's liven things up with some pretty faces. No one wants to see Herbert Von Metzenberg in the morning paper— spoil breakfast."

"Von Metzenberg?" Paisley suddenly appeared at Kelly's side. "Here? Today?"

"Any minute. Stick around, Paisley. You can be in the shot, too."

"I sure will," Paisley purred. "Herbert Von Metzenberg is the sponsor of the benefit—he's loaded! And powerful, too—it wouldn't hurt to get to know him personally, if you catch my drift."

Uneasily, Kelly watched Alex while he arranged the spotlights to find the most flattering lighting in the huge, open room.

"Paisley didn't mean that the way it sounded," she whispered to Alex. "About Von Metzenberg."

"You're a good friend to stick up for her like that." Alex stepped back, nodding appreciatively at Kelly, who was bathed in a halo of bright light.

"Hey, Michelangelo," Steve barked. "Nothing so artsy, okay? This is a straightforward publicity shot—just light it so we can see it. No special effects, okay?" Grumpily, Steve continued to mutter under his breath. "Publicity shots—hack work . . . junk . . . waste of time . . ."

Kelly felt embarrassed for Alex, to be yelled at like that in front of people. But Alex just winked at her and calmly readjusted the lights.

"Why *is* Steve doing these shots?" she whispered.

"When Von Metzenberg whistles, you jump," Alex whispered back. "His people won't okay ordinary publicity photos."

Suddenly there was a rush of activity: the ballroom doors swung open and a troop of people marched in, all of them in dark business suits and all looking very important.

"Mr. Von Metzenberg," Steve gushed with a giant, phony smile on his face. "So nice to see you, sir. Right this way, please . . . We won't take a minute of your time."

"Good—my time is valuable," answered a sweet-looking old man.

Paisley kept tossing her bright shawl over one shoulder, then the other, obviously nervous in the company of such an important person. The businessmen anxiously surrounded Mr. Von Metzenberg, offering pens, cigars, matches—Kelly couldn't see what all the fuss was about. *Herbert Von Metzenberg looks perfectly nice*, she thought.

Kelly liked his snowy mustache and white hair combed in an old-fashioned style. She thought she detected a twinkle in his eye. Steve was bowing and scraping all over the place, but Mr. Von Metzenberg reminded Kelly of—of Santa Claus! Meg's comparison struck her as so appropriate that she giggled.

Von Metzenberg turned to see who was laughing at him.

"What's so funny?" he demanded, and Kelly felt the steel behind those kindly eyes. For a moment she lost her nerve completely. But she wasn't about to act terrified, like Paisley, or to practically drool over him, like Steve.

"I was laughing at you," she began bravely. Immediately, everyone in the room stiffened, and she regretted her impulse to speak the truth. But in the corner of her eye, she could see Alex nod at her to say what she felt.

"You reminded me of someone, and then I realized who it was," she continued, while Steve and Paisley watched her, horror on their faces.

"Who?" Von Metzenberg demanded.

Kelly swallowed. "Santa Claus!"

To her relief and astonishment, Von Metzenberg's face broke out in a grin. "Santa Claus," he repeated and laughed heartily. "I like that—you know, young lady," he said, taking Kelly's arm confidentially, "to lots of people—my stockholders, for example—I *am* Santa Claus." He turned to his assistants. "Isn't that right?"

"Yessir, Mr. Von Metzenberg," they answered in chorus.

He dismissed them with a wave of his hand. "Santa Claus," he said again, chuckling.

Nervously, Steve approached. "Er, Mr. Von Metzenberg, if you could just stand here—with Kelly and Paisley, if you don't mind—we'll get this over with."

"What's the big rush?" Von Metzenberg demanded. "Don't push me around like a puppet." He peered frankly at Kelly. "Who are you? Tell me about herself."

Dutifully, Kelly began telling him about her family in Franklyn, the cross-country team, and being discovered by Meg Dorian. Although everyone else seemed either bored or impatient, Von Metzenberg listened attentively to everything she had to say.

"A model and an athlete," he said when she had finished. "Interesting combination."

"And a student, too," Kelly added.

One of the assistants stepped forward to remind Von Metzenberg about an upcoming appointment.

"Time is money," Von Metzenberg said, looking right at Steve. "Why are we wasting it?"

Steve's eyes widened, his face reddened, but he didn't dare say anything back to Von Metzenberg. Kelly smiled to herself, he looked so comical; but Alex laughed out loud. Steve looked like he would fire Alex on the spot for laughing at him, but Von Metzenberg interfered.

"You—with the strange sense of humor," Von Metzenberg said to Alex. "Don't I know you? What's your name?"

"Alex Hawkins."

"Know your father, don't I?"

"Yes, sir, you do," Alex answered politely.

Kelly was astounded. Alex's father must be pretty important for a man like Von Metzenberg to know who he was. When Steve said Alex was a rich kid, he hadn't been kidding. Still, Alex seemed so natural and ordinary; Kelly couldn't quite believe his background could be that different from hers.

"Let's get this show on the road," Steve commanded. "Set it up, Hawkins."

Alex positioned Kelly, Von Metzenberg, and

Paisley under the bright lights, winking at Kelly when they were in place. Kelly answered his wink with a broad smile. He really was a nice person.

The photographs were taken quickly and everyone congratulated everyone else on how smoothly it had gone, as if they had really accomplished something important. Alex began packing up Steve's equipment while Steve spoke hurriedly to Von Metzenberg's assistants, arranging for the photos to be delivered to the proper newspapers and publicity people.

"You really moved in fast," Paisley told Kelly coldly.

Kelly, who was carefully repacking her makeup into her model's kit, didn't understand at first. "Moved in?" she repeated.

"Don't act so innocent," Paisley said scornfully. "*Santa Claus.* Very cute, Kelly."

"What are you talking about?" Kelly looked up, astounded at the angry tears in Paisley's eyes.

"You know how important this whole thing is to me. I wanted Von Metzenberg to notice *me.* Don't pretend you didn't do it on purpose—you were horrible, flirting with him like that, stealing all the attention."

"I didn't mean to," Kelly protested. "Paisley, I wasn't trying to cut you out."

"You don't need Von Metzenberg, you don't need this whole benefit show. But I do. As soon as I have the backers, I intend to go into business for myself. 'Paisley Designs' has been a dream of mine for as long as I can remember. I already got Clyde Mason to notice me. If I had Von Metzenberg to back me, I'd be practically all set to go. Clyde would design his next line around the 'Paisley Look,' and Von Metzenberg could introduce me to society; I'd be famous overnight! But you step in and ruin everything."

"Paisley, come on, I didn't know!" Awkwardly, Kelly reached for the other girl, but Paisley twisted away. "I didn't know you were a designer, you should have said something . . ."

"You didn't give me a chance to say anything," Paisley accused hotly. "And then, as soon as you found out that Alex is rich, and Von Metzenberg knows his father, you went after him, too!"

"That's unfair," Kelly cried. "Alex seems like a nice guy, but I'm not after him. As a matter of fact, I like someone else . . ."

"You like anyone you can use!"

Now Kelly was getting angry. "That's not true, I'm not like that," she insisted. "I'm sorry things didn't work out for you today, but I didn't do anything purposely to hurt you. I'm not competing with you, Paisley."

"Tell it to Von Metzenberg," Paisley snapped. She glared at Kelly angrily, wiping a tear from her cheek. "I thought we could be friends, but I should have known—you can't trust anybody in this business. I'll show you someday, when I'm famous—and I'll be famous, without your help or anyone else's!"

"Wait a minute. Aren't you overreacting?" Kelly faced her patiently. "One meeting isn't going to make or break your career. Von Metzenberg just met you today—so on Monday, call his office and speak to him. Isn't that the way to start in business?"

"That's the way if you have pull," Paisley snapped angrily. "Sure, Alex Hawkins could get to him—he's rich, Von Metzenberg knows his father. But I'm nobody, from nowhere. A busy man isn't going to take time to talk to me. Meeting him today was a stroke of fantastic luck, and just when I'm ready to make my move, you butt in with your wide-eyed innocent act and steal the show!"

"I didn't do it on purpose," Kelly insisted. "Come on, Paisley, forget it. We have to work together. Let's be friends."

"Honey, that's either the best con job I've ever heard, or you're too sickeningly sweet to be true. Either way, forget it. I don't need friends like you."

Helplessly, Kelly watched while Paisley stormed out of the ballroom. She was so confused she didn't know whether to feel angry or hurt— she just knew she felt miserable.

Alex came over to her. "We're about set to leave," he said pleasantly, "and I thought, maybe . . ." He looked closely at her face. "Hey, what's wrong?"

"Nothing." Kelly shook her head. She couldn't even tell Alex about it: he might think Paisley's accusations were true—that Kelly had been trying to flirt with Von Metzenberg, and with Alex, too, because of their money and connections. Plenty of girls would use modeling as a chance to meet handsome, wealthy men; it wasn't unheard of.

And Kelly had just defended Paisley to Alex; how could she suddenly turn on her, tell Alex that Paisley had accused her of terrible things? Alex would surely think Kelly was crazy, or a liar, or a rotten friend herself. There was no way to explain anything without ruining Alex's good opinion of her, and for some reason, his opinion really mattered.

"Something happened," Alex said. "I'll bet Paisley got jealous of you, didn't she?"

Kelly started. "Why do you think that?"

"It isn't hard to figure out," Alex assured her. "You made a big hit with Von Metzenberg, and anyone could see that Paisley was trying her best to impress him."

"I didn't mean to," Kelly said. "I'm not a flirt, and I don't use people. I'm just not like that."

"Hey," Alex answered, his voice kind and understanding, "you can't help it if Metzy liked you. You were just being yourself, and most people aren't natural around him. He scares everyone to death."

"Metzy?" Kelly smiled; she couldn't imagine anyone calling important, powerful Herbert Von Metzenberg by that silly nickname.

"He and my dad went to school together," Alex explained, "and that's what everyone called him then."

"I would never be able to call him that," Kelly said.

"If anyone could, you could." Alex laughed. "Listen, Kelly—you're a straightforward, honest girl; that's why Metzy liked you. Anyone would like you. So don't let anything Paisley said get to you too much. You're great the way you are."

Kelly beamed. "Thanks. I guess I do let other people get to me too much sometimes. I tend to take things too seriously, but . . ."

But Steve Hollender interrupted the conversation. "Hawkins, I'm not paying you to score with the ladies—how about earning your pay?"

Kelly called a quick goodbye and headed for home, repeating Alex's words over in her mind all the way back to the bus terminal, on the bus, and at the bus stop as she waited for her mother to pick her up. It really helped that Alex believed she hadn't tricked Paisley. Kelly wasn't the kind of girl to take advantage of a friend, and it hurt that Paisley thought differently.

Somehow, I'll get things straight with Paisley, she vowed. It would be nice to have a friend who was also a model, who understood what she was going through, what her new life was like. It was important. Somehow, telling Jennifer or her other friends about her new career wasn't enough. She needed someone to share things with, someone who understood when Kelly was exhausted from a shoot—someone who didn't think she was spoiled and that modeling was really a lark. Sure, Jennifer tried to sympathize with Kelly, but talking to her wasn't the same as talking to someone who had been through it herself.

Paisley took the time to help me with the runway show; she was a friend, Kelly thought. *Her accusations were unfair, but that's because Paisley doesn't know me well enough to trust me yet; it was just a misunderstanding.* Kelly couldn't stand to have Paisley thinking the worst about her; she couldn't stand to have anyone think she'd done something she hadn't done. Kelly would convince Paisley she'd been wrong; she had to.

But if Paisley didn't believe me, Alex did. Kelly could count Alex on her side; and that thought was comforting—and strangely exciting.

Six

Jennifer bounded up the stairs, yelling for Kelly
and waving a newspaper excitedly.

"Kelly—you're in the paper, did you see? You
look great!"

She burst into Kelly's room to find Kelly
peering through her curtains at the house across
the street.

"Kelly—did you hear me? Your picture's in the
paper!"

"Sssh!" Kelly warned, waving Jennifer back
from the window. "Eric's out there. He washed
his car this morning and now he's getting ready to
go somewhere. . . . Do you think he has a
date?"

"I couldn't care less." Jennifer threw herself
onto Kelly's bed, spreading the newspaper out in
front of her.

"Jen!" Kelly was shocked. Jennifer had always

been on her side when it came to Eric—more than once, Jennifer had spied on Eric through Kelly's window, every bit as interested as her best friend in his activities. That's what a best friend was for. "I think it must be a date," Kelly said. "Why else would he wash his car?"

"Maybe because it was filthy." Jennifer shuddered. "You should have seen the rotting junk in the backseat. I thought he was growing mold back there."

"When were you in Eric's car?" Kelly immediately felt a stab of jealousy.

"Yesterday after school, while you were at your rehearsal. A bunch of us went to the library to study. Eric stopped by later and gave us all a ride home." Jennifer turned the pages of the newspaper rapidly, searching for Kelly's picture. "I meant to tell you all about it on the phone last night, but when I heard your news I forgot. And don't worry," she added, "Eric doesn't have a date. We all gave him such a hard time about his disgusting car that he had to wash it before appearing in public again."

"Who was at the library?" Kelly tried to sound casual. Across the street, Eric got into his car and drove off. "Anyone special?"

"Here it is," Jennifer cried, pointing out the picture Steve had taken the previous afternoon. "You and that model Paisley and your pal Metzy." She giggled. "He *does* look like Santa Claus."

Kelly left the window and put her hand over the newspaper photo. "Who was there yesterday?" she repeated.

"Oh, no one special," Jennifer assured her. "No one Eric is interested in, if that's what you mean. It was strictly platonic. Though he did ask where you were," she added merrily, showing both her dimples.

"He did?" Kelly flopped down on the bed beside Jennifer. "What did he say? Tell me every word."

"He said, 'Where's Kelly?'" Jennifer teased. "He also said they missed you at cross-country practice, and that he hoped you weren't too busy modeling to stay on the team."

"He said all that, about me? He actually missed me, Jen—he worried that I wasn't around yesterday. I may be getting to that boy after all." She grabbed Jennifer's arm. "Did he seem sad I wasn't there, or was he just being polite?"

"I don't know—I guess he was more than polite."

"That's great!" Kelly smiled dreamily.

"Then you're still interested in Eric—despite that new boy you met yesterday?"

Kelly frowned. "Alex Hawkins? Alex was really nice to me, but I'm not giving up on Eric. Besides, I never dated a college boy before and he probably wouldn't be interested in me."

"You are so naive," Jennifer groaned. "Steve Hollender was interested in you, and he's ancient."

Kelly shuddered. "Don't remind me. I think Steve would take out any pretty girl, just to be seen with her. Eric's more my style."

"Eric—at a time like this? In just a few hours you'll be at the Children's Fund Benefit Ball, dazzling movie stars with your fresh beauty. That's what it says here, anyway."

Kelly looked at the newspaper photo and quickly read the caption, which described her and Paisley as "two of the fresh young beauties who promise to dazzle a host of celebrities with Clyde

Mason's fabulous fashions at tonight's exclusive Children's Fund Benefit Ball."

"I can see you now," Jennifer sighed, "dancing all night in the arms of some fabulously handsome young man—like Alex Hawkins."

"Or stumbling around with Metzy Metzenberg," Kelly cracked. "Seriously, Jen—I won't be dancing in anyone's arms. I'm not exactly a guest, you know; I'm working tonight. In fact, the fashion show will be over long before the dancing starts."

"That stinks," Jennifer said. "I pictured you in some spectacular gown, dancing till dawn. I can't believe it."

"Believe it. First of all, these dresses are exclusive Clyde Mason designs—no one has seen them yet, not even me, and I'm going to be wearing them! Tonight is the grand unveiling, and after we model the dresses, they go right back to Clyde's showroom." She shrugged. "So you see, I'll be in my jeans, and I could hardly go dancing that way."

"Then wear your own dress," Jennifer urged. "You'll still look beautiful."

"I can't, Jen. First of all, this is a formal affair, and I don't own a ballgown. Besides, even if I had the right kind of dress, you have to pay a lot of money to get in. They won't let us anywhere near the ball."

"I guess it doesn't matter," Jennifer said, though she hardly seemed convinced. "I guess those movie stars wouldn't be interested in a sixteen-year-old girl, anyway."

"What are you going to do tonight?" Kelly asked. "I should be home by ten—want to sleep over?"

"No thanks. I want to get to bed early tonight—I've got so much work to do, thanks to my computer exam."

"You always get A's," Kelly reminded her. "I'm the one who should be worried—about catching up in biology."

"Are you?"

"No—I can't stop thinking about tonight," Kelly admitted. "I'm still nervous about the whole thing. Here I am, an athlete, and I'm terrified of my wobbly ankles and of falling off my three-inch heels!"

Jennifer ended up staying for lunch, which was a blessing, because Kelly's mother and her sister were so excited about the fashion show that Jennifer was the only one acting halfway normal. As soon as they could, the two girls escaped upstairs, where Kelly washed her hair and tried to decide if she should pin it up or leave it loose and natural.

"I'd better leave it," Kelly said, "in case they want a special look."

"What about your makeup?" Jennifer was plowing through Kelly's model's kit, where she kept an assortment of about thirty different eye shadows, as well as makeup base, powder, blushes, mascara, eyeliner, and assorted brushes to apply it all.

"I'll do my face here," Kelly said thoughtfully, "so even if they want some kind of special look I'll have the basics already on."

"This whole thing sounds so disorganized," Jennifer said. "I always thought they did all your makeup for you, like in make-over pictures in the magazines."

Kelly smiled ruefully. "Not always—and you have to learn fast. I was no expert at makeup, and my first catalog shoot was a nightmare. No one bothered to tell me how to use enough makeup to look natural but not overdone, and my pictures were practically useless. I had no lips or eyes at all."

Jennifer studied her own face in the mirror. "How does this look? I didn't use any shadow on the lid, just in the crease."

"It looks beautiful," Kelly said sincerely, because Jennifer *was* beautiful. Her best friend was always perfectly dressed and made up—much more so than Kelly had ever been. In fact, if Jennifer had been taller, *she* would have been the one discovered by Meg Dorian; Kelly was positive of it.

Sometimes Kelly still wasn't sure she was doing the right thing—clothes and makeup were second nature to some girls, like Jennifer, but Kelly had always been more the tomboy type, impatient when her mother told her to comb her hair before going out. Kelly knew she was doing quite well in her career, yet she had so many doubts; she dreaded doing things wrong.

Now is no time to worry about it, she told herself.

"Help me get this foundation smooth," she said aloud, and she and Jennifer worked on her face until they thought Kelly was about as made up as anyone could be.

"I think it looks perfect," Jennifer announced, stepping back after an hour's work. "We put a lot on, but this is a dressy occasion, isn't it?"

"I think so," Kelly said doubtfully. She thought

they might have overdone it; but she could always wipe some off if she had to.

Her mother knocked at the door, poking her head inside. "Are you ready, honey? The car's going to be here any minute."

"The agency is sending a car for me tonight," Kelly explained. "They don't usually, but Meg feels tonight is important and she wants to be sure I get there relaxed and on time."

"Meg really keeps tabs on you," Jennifer remarked.

"Sometimes it's as if Kelly's got an extra mother," Mrs. Blake agreed.

"She's a smart businesswoman," Kelly said. "It's the same as someone keeping track of stocks and bonds—to Meg, I'm an investment."

Mrs. Blake marveled at her daughter's composure. "I don't know where you learn these things," she said in admiration. "You make me feel so ignorant sometimes."

"Oh, Mom," Kelly said. "Just wish me luck tonight."

Mrs. Blake kissed her daughter. "You look beautiful, honey, though I wish you'd wear a nice skirt instead of those jeans. What will Meg think?"

"All the girls wear jeans. Really, Mom—no one dresses up for assignments. I'll be fine."

"If you're sure," Mrs. Blake said doubtfully. "Do you have everything?"

"Uh-huh." Smiling with Jennifer at her mother's hovering concern, Kelly walked to the sidewalk. "Let's wait for the car here," she said. "So I won't have to listen to my mother worry over me."

"So you can see if Eric came home yet, you mean."

In a few minutes, Eric's car did pull into his driveway, and waving hello, Eric leaped out and crossed the street.

"Just who I wanted to see," he called out cheerfully. "I just spent a worthless afternoon at the library. Everyone was horsing around so much I didn't get any studying done. How about a study party tonight, Kelly? We could get a lot done."

Kelly's heart sank. An invitation from Eric, and she couldn't accept. Not that studying was a date, exactly, but it was the best offer she'd had from him lately.

"I'd love to, Eric," she began, just as the shiny black limousine sent by the FLASH! agency appeared around the corner.

"Kelly Blake?" the driver asked.

"That's me," she answered. "Could you wait a minute?"

The driver looked meaningfully at his watch—no doubt Meg had ordered "no waiting time," but Kelly couldn't let Eric's offer—and Eric—away from her.

"Eric, I'd really love to study with you, but I have a job tonight."

Eric eyed the shiny black limousine. "I can see you have better things to do."

He looked so uncomfortable that Kelly had to put him more at ease.

"This is just like a taxi," she said. "Really—it's no big deal."

Jennifer chimed in. "It's for that fashion show—the charity benefit; Kelly's modeling tonight."

The driver tapped on the window, pointing to his watch.

"I have a great idea," Jennifer suddenly said. "Why don't you and I study together tonight, Eric? We could both use some work before that programming exam."

Eric's eyes practically lit up. "Hey, that would be great."

Kelly felt a slight shock. "I thought you were planning an early night tonight?"

"But this way," Jennifer said, "Eric and I can help each other, and if you get home early enough, you can come over . . ."

"Honey, wait," Judith Blake called from the house. She and Tina ran down to the sidewalk to give Kelly another big hug and a kiss goodbye. "I brought you a warmer jacket," her mother said. "It'll be cold out later." She began fussing with Kelly's hair. "Shouldn't you have done something more to your hair?"

"My hair is fine," Kelly snapped. She opened the back door of the limousine before the driver had a chance to get out and open it for her. *I'm not a princess, after all*, she thought, and ignored the jacket her mother thrust at her.

"Sure, you guys study together. What do I care?" The limousine pulled away from the curb, and Kelly leaned out the window. "I have better things to do tonight, important things—like raising money for sick children!"

She collapsed against the car seat. She was furious and hurt; how could Jennifer do that to her? Kelly wanted to be with Eric tonight—it wasn't her fault she had this stupid job. And Jennifer hadn't helped any, raving about the limousine and Kelly's career when she knew perfectly well Eric wasn't overly impressed by Kelly's modeling. Jennifer had done everything she could to ruin Kelly's chances with him!

The driver spoke over his shoulder. "Was that friend of yours a model, too? The Chinese girl, I mean."

"No, Jennifer's not a model. She's way too short," Kelly pointed out.

"Yeah, I can see that," the driver answered. "She was pretty, though, and she seemed like a nice girl, too. Seemed proud of you, that's for sure."

"She's my best friend," Kelly answered, though she certainly didn't feel like Jennifer's best friend anymore. Suppose Eric liked Jennifer better than her? Suppose he thought Kelly was too stuck-up to waste time with? Kelly grimaced, remembering her parting words: "I have better things to do tonight." *I should learn to keep my big mouth shut.*

Leaning against the cushions, she sighed. She felt like Cinderella, like a poor girl all dressed up, riding in a coach about to turn into a pumpkin. She shouldn't be in this limousine, anyway; she really wanted to be crowded around a kitchen table drinking Cokes, eating chips, and cracking jokes. She was no fairy-tale princess—she was Kelly Blake, an ordinary high-school girl from New Jersey. She sighed again, and the driver looked at her in the rearview mirror.

"Too hot in the car, miss?"

"No, no, it's fine," she said hurriedly. *Sometimes life is so complicated!*

Seven

Kelly couldn't stop thinking about Jennifer studying alone with Eric that night. She had blown it, all right. She wouldn't blame Jennifer for never speaking to her again, and Eric would certainly never ask her to do anything with him after this. The sad thing was that her rude comment hadn't been true: she didn't think the benefit show was more important than studying and she would rather be with Eric tonight than anywhere else. But it was hopeless now. She might as well forget Eric Powers.

The chauffeur spoke again. "This is a big celebrity affair tonight, isn't it? My wife was reading about it in the paper."

"Pretty big," Kelly answered without much enthusiasm. "But I won't be anywhere near the celebrities. I'm just going to be in the fashion show. I have to leave before the dance even starts."

"Yeah? That's too bad. But it must be great, at your age, working for important people, being a model."

"I guess it is pretty exciting," Kelly answered.

The only trouble was, as soon as she admitted how exciting the benefit was, she also started getting nervous. About being in the same room with so many famous people, about walking the wrong way, about offending the other models somehow, about everything. "Just copy the girl in front of you," Paisley had said—but Kelly had had a tough time copying Paisley.

Her stomach churned at the thought of seeing Paisley again. She had to get things straight between them, but Paisley probably wouldn't listen. *Oh, well,* Kelly told herself, *it doesn't matter what Paisley thinks.* Kelly knew she wasn't an opportunist; she didn't use people.

But it did matter. Kelly was the type of girl who hated to have anyone think badly of her—especially when what they thought wasn't true. She'd been like that ever since she was a little kid; when her parents punished her for something she didn't do, Kelly would flip out. The worst fight they'd ever had happened when Tina accused Kelly of hiding her favorite stuffed animal. Their parents were furious—Tina was in tears, and she really did look pathetic, but no one believed Kelly didn't know where Fluffy was. It was one of the few times Kelly had ever been spanked, and she went to bed hating everyone in her family.

The next day, when Fluffy turned up in the laundry hamper mixed up with Tina's pajamas (which Tina had thrown there herself), everyone suddenly believed Kelly was innocent and apologized repeatedly. But no matter how much her parents apologized and tried to make it up to her, Kelly never totally forgave them.

She knew it would be the same with Paisley, unless she made Paisley believe the truth.

The driver maneuvered the long car to a parking space in front of the hotel, and Kelly got out, dragging her model's kit along the ground.

"Let's see a pretty smile," the driver said as she walked away.

A sickly grin was all she could manage. How would she ever get through this night?

The elevator opened onto the Starlight Roof. Although it was nearly time for the fashion show to begin, the room was half empty, and Kelly suspected many of the guests would arrive "fashionably" late. She headed for the back hallway where Vanessa had said the dressing room would be, turned the corner, and suddenly was in the midst of utter chaos.

"Kelly!" Vanessa appeared, waving frantically. "This way." She gave Kelly a push—toward the hairdresser, Kelly assumed—and then disappeared.

Kelly stripped down to her T-shirt and jeans and sat in front of a brightly lit makeup mirror. The hairdresser, Reed, fussed over her.

"This hair," he moaned, "there's so much of it!" He reached over the table strewn with rollers and hair clips, blow dryers, curling irons, and a waffle stick to put ripples in hair.

Kelly saw a big, shiny pair of scissors and she screamed nervously, "Don't cut my hair!"

Everyone turned to stare, and Reed gave her an indignant look. "I wasn't about to cut these disgusting tresses," he said archly. "There isn't time. But look around you—get the idea?"

Kelly looked: immediately she understood why Reed was so upset. Every model had an extremely short haircut; every model but her.

"It's the balance," Reed explained. "Long hair will throw off the line of the clothes—Clyde will die when he sees you. I can try wrapping it tight to your scalp."

"What about a French twist?" Kelly said. She held her hair up in back and twisted it; you could hardly tell it wasn't short hair.

"No, no," Reed groaned, "the balance is all wrong. I'm going to mousse everyone's hair out straight . . ."

Kelly giggled. She had put her hair up hundreds of times, and she thought Reed was overreacting. What was the big deal? Somehow, the more agitated Reed got, the calmer Kelly got, forgetting her nervousness.

While Reed complained, Kelly took a moment to look around backstage. Models were everywhere, in makeup robes, in slips, even in their underwear, getting last-minute instructions from Vanessa and the other assistants.

At last Reed began pinning and twisting Kelly's hair in a hundred separate pincurls all over her head. He left an inch of hair loose at each end, slathering on the mousse and pulling the ends out straight from her head. At first Kelly giggled; she looked like a reject from a horror movie. Then she started to feel uncomfortable.

"Am I really going out there in front of people like this?" she asked. It hardly seemed possible; her mother, so fond of Kelly's long, thick hair, would die if she saw her now. She looked like a weirdo, a freak.

"Listen, honey, it's the best I can do," Reed snapped. "You should have cut it off." He looked at his watch. "Let's finish this."

To Kelly's horror, Reed grabbed a can of green tint and began squirting a swatch of color onto her head.

"What are you doing?" she shrieked.

Reed glared at her. "It's an outer-space theme," he snarled. "Don't you know anything? Look around you."

Kelly looked. Sure enough, the other girls had been transformed into strange, exotic creatures: each spiky head had a stripe of bright color, and each face had been painted on one side with the same color stripe. From the left they looked completely normal, and quite beautiful; but from the right, the color stripe went from each model's hair, down her forehead, around her eye, and over her cheek.

It was worse than Kelly had imagined when she'd seen Clyde's ads in the magazine; and green hair just wasn't her type. Obviously, Reed thought so, too.

"I don't know," Kelly said doubtfully. "Green hair?"

"We have to do it," Reed said. He sprayed generously; it would take forever to wash the green tint out. "Okay, we're running late; better get to makeup."

"Makeup?" Kelly couldn't believe it. "I have an inch of makeup on already," she complained, thinking how hard she and Jennifer had worked for a glamorous evening look.

"Just go to makeup." Reed whisked the towel from around her neck, and Kelly obediently walked over to the makeup table. The excitement backstage reminded her of the times she had been in school plays and dance recitals. She was still anxious about her hair, but in a way the anxiety only made her look forward to the fashion show. Maybe she *was* right for this business after all.

Her hair might look ridiculous, but the other girls looked stunning. The colors had been applied skillfully, as if each girl were a painting in a different color. She almost didn't mind when the makeup girl destroyed the careful job she and Jennifer had slaved over.

A careful, jagged stripe was drawn on her right cheek in black, and then the makeup girl, Laureen, filled in the area with a green that matched the shade in Kelly's hair. Her right eye was magnificent: Laureen outlined it first in black, then in shiny gold. Kelly's eyelid and brow bone were painted white and then filled in with delicate areas of pink.

"The details won't show from a distance," Laureen explained, "but they add depth to the effect."

"It's beautiful," Kelly admitted. "I look like some strange flower."

Laureen added a tiny amount of glitter along the outline on Kelly's right cheek. "Enough to catch the lights," she explained, "without looking like glitter." The end result was surprisingly attractive, and except for the silly corkscrew hairdo, Kelly thought she looked sensational.

"The best one is my redhead," Laureen said. "Paisley. That hair of hers is such a fabulous color—I did her face dead-white. Very dramatic. Clyde will love it."

Paisley. Kelly had almost forgotten about her, and now she hated to think about their meeting. Maybe they wouldn't even bump into each other tonight—but that didn't seem very likely.

"Paisley *is* very pretty," she said, because Laureen seemed to be waiting for her to say something in response.

"And talented, too," Laureen said. "She especially wanted to look good tonight. You know she does those sketches—dress designs. Well, she brought them tonight to show Clyde. I thought maybe she shouldn't bother him—he doesn't like being bothered by anyone—but you can't tell Paisley anything. And she was so excited I didn't have the heart to stop her. I just hope she doesn't get her feelings hurt."

For a second, Kelly almost felt glad that Paisley's feelings would be hurt. But if what Laureen said was true, disturbing Clyde Mason with her sketches would get Paisley into big trouble. Not only would the famous designer get angry, but if word got back to Meg that Paisley had made a pest of herself, Paisley might never get another live modeling job again. If Kelly really wanted to be Paisley's friend, she would have to rescue her; convince her that tonight was the wrong time to bother Clyde.

Kelly was torn. If she was going to do anything, she had better do it fast. She could let Paisley walk into the trap of bothering Clyde, or she could follow her best instincts and try to stop her.

With one eye on the clock, Kelly glanced around the dressing room for a sign of Paisley and Clyde Mason. They didn't seem to be anywhere. Then, just as Kelly was getting ready to find Vanessa to learn what her first outfit would be, she spied Paisley.

Outrageously made up and wearing a plain white robe, Paisley was sitting behind a covered rack of dresses, balancing a drawing portfolio on her knees. Kelly took a deep breath and made her decision.

"Paisley, I've got to talk to you," Kelly said.

"Not you." Paisley sprang up. "Go away, Kelly—you'll ruin everything. You've done enough harm."

"But Laureen told me what you're going to do. It's bad timing! She said you shouldn't bother Clyde tonight. He's worried about the show and he won't care about your sketches—you'll just make him angry, and then he'll never take you seriously."

Paisley gave her an icy look. "Look, Clyde Mason already knows who I am. He remembered me from last year, and this is my best chance to nab him. My work is great, but I'll never get an appointment to show my sketches at his office; I've tried. So it's now or never." Her eyes narrowed suspiciously. "Why do you care, anyway—why don't you want Clyde to see my drawings?"

"I do want him to see them, but not now," Kelly pleaded. "Forget what happened yesterday. Please believe me, I'm trying to help you."

"Help? Why would you help me? What are you after—don't tell me you're a fashion designer, too!"

Kelly groaned. "It's nothing like that. If you'd only let me explain about yesterday."

"Yesterday you showed your true colors." Paisley turned her back.

"You've got me all wrong. Believe me, I don't care about Metzy Metzenberg."

"Metzy?" Paisley whirled around, her eyes opened wide. "You're calling him nicknames now—you really do work fast."

This is hopeless, Kelly thought to herself. Taking a deep breath, she plunged into her explanation. "Von Metzenberg noticed me because I wasn't afraid of him," she said, "not because I was trying to get his attention. I just want to be a good model, nothing more. I hate it when someone holds me responsible for something I didn't do. Please believe me, Paisley—I'm not the type who uses people."

"You all look splendid!" A booming voice rang out, and Kelly saw Paisley stiffen: it was Clyde Mason—a very dramatic figure. For the formal occasion, Clyde wore an elegant evening suit, beautifully cut and quite conservative in outline, except that the fabric was a fabulous, startling white velvet. He looked completely outrageous but totally at ease. Kelly had stopped talking, dazzled by Clyde's forceful presence. She didn't see how Paisley—or anyone—would have the nerve to speak to him.

"You're all my special girls tonight, and I love you," he told everyone assembled backstage. "We're going to knock them dead!"

They all cheered, and Kelly felt the thrill of belonging to a special group. Clyde knew how to create excitement, that was clear. She could hardly wait to put on one of his dresses and show it to the world.

"Clyde, I have something to show you." A bit breathlessly Paisley pushed her way to Clyde's side, ignoring Vanessa, who was frantically organizing the girls into their first costumes and accessories. The air was filled with gasps of admiration as the exclusive dresses were removed from their bags for the first time—yet Kelly was only half paying attention, she was so concerned about Paisley.

"Clyde, I love it!" Adrianne, the willowy blond Kelly had often seen in Clyde Mason's magazine ads, stood revealed in a shimmering fantasy of bright, intense blue. The material clung to her body in wispy layers—sometimes thick and deep, sometimes so thin they were almost transparent. Kelly gasped. It was the most beautiful dress she had ever seen. It sparkled and shone with a thousand tiny diamonds, and when an assistant set a crown of three stark feathers on Adrianne's head, Kelly understood the special excitement of the event. The fantasy headpiece joined the painted stripe of Adrianne's hair and the streak of color on her face to complete the illusion: Adrianne was a goddess from another planet. Everyone, models and stylists, was silent in admiration for a moment, and then an excited babble broke out.

"It's my most daring collection ever," Clyde said proudly. "Star Children and Moon Maidens— I told you, we're going to make fashion history tonight."

The models crowded around Vanessa, demanding to see which gowns they were to wear. An argument even broke out, as two equally stunning models insisted that one particular dress was "made for me alone." Any pretense of calm disappeared. Everyone was involved in sorting out the dresses—everyone but Paisley, that is.

She approached Clyde again, imploring him to look at her sketches.

"I've got daytime and sportswear in front," Paisley was saying, holding the portfolio under Clyde's nose, "and formal wear in back. See, I used one color theme . . ."

"Yes, uh, nice . . . very nice." Clyde craned his head over Paisley's shoulder, trying to keep an eye on the backstage chaos.

"I was very influenced by you," Paisley almost shouted, trying to be heard above the racket. "I remembered what you said about unity of line and color . . ."

"Great, sweetheart . . . Adrianne, don't fidget—those seams are delicate . . ."

Paisley was almost in tears, desperately struggling for Clyde's attention. "The formals are the best, here—see these?"

She thrust the portfolio up to Clyde's face and he instinctively threw up an arm, knocking the drawings out of Paisley's hand. They fell to the floor, sliding and slithering around in a messy pile.

"My drawings!" Paisley cried, stooping to gather them up before they were trampled.

"Look out," Kelly yelled, as Clyde took a step backward and almost tripped over the sketches. Just in time, she snatched three of Paisley's most delicate watercolors from under his feet and brushed off the soiled sketches, smoothing out the battered edges.

"Look what you've done," Paisley wailed, tears of frustration escaping down her cheeks. "They're ruined, ruined!"

Clyde stared, anxious to stop the commotion

backstage and totally bewildered by Paisley and Kelly.

"What is going on?" he sputtered. Then he spotted Kelly, and did a double take. He reached out and grabbed her by the shoulders, shaking her a bit roughly.

"What's happened to this girl's hair?" he demanded in a fury. All noise stopped as everyone turned to look at him. Kelly cringed: Clyde's grip was so tight it hurt. She stared at him, bewildered and frightened.

"Reed! Vanessa!" Clyde exploded. "Who's responsible for this?"

"I'm sorry—what did I do . . ." Kelly looked from Clyde to Paisley, stricken with anxiety and terribly confused.

Reed and Vanessa appeared. Reed was clearly bewildered by Clyde's anger, but Vanessa gasped when she saw Kelly.

"Isn't this Kelly Blake, the new girl from FLASH!?" Clyde asked coldly.

"Yes—oh, Clyde! I sent her to makeup and she must have gone to Reed instead . . ."

Clyde turned on Reed. "Who told you to do her hair that way? It's terrible, awful—don't you people understand anything—what do I pay you for?"

Clyde delivered a stinging tirade about the incompetents he was surrounded with. "Nothing is right! Ruined, all ruined!" He began pulling the pin curls out of Kelly's hair.

Reed and Vanessa seemed to be too familiar with Clyde's angry explosions to interfere. They stood by while Clyde yanked out the pin curls, pulling out some of Kelly's hair as well. When

Kelly tried to protect her head, he pushed her hands away, until every last bobby pin was out of her hair. Kelly was mortified; she wished she could sink into the ground. She didn't understand at all—what had she done wrong?

Eight

"There—now maybe we can start over," Clyde said crossly. "We have about two minutes to fix the inevitable blunders."

"Blunders?" Kelly said helplessly.

Vanessa spoke up. "Kelly, this is partly my fault. Your hair was supposed to be different, but then Reed got hold of you . . ."

"What?" Kelly turned from one to the other. "Would someone please tell me what's happening?" She had a terrible feeling she had done something wrong.

Paisley gave Kelly a sly grin; at least Paisley wasn't the only one in trouble now.

"You were supposed to be my Earth Maiden," Clyde said. "You see, most of these dresses are fantasy creations, more for show than for actual wearing: entertainment value, to make the benefit a success. But several of the dresses will be in my spring line, and tonight is the public's first chance to view them. To set those off, I wanted a girl strikingly different from the rest."

"That's right," Vanessa agreed. "You'll come out at the end of each set, your hair dark and full, in contrast to the short haircuts, and you'll be wearing a special dress. It's a smashing effect—we've done it before. I should have been watching you especially closely, to see that your hair and makeup were what Clyde wanted."

"Well, no one told me," Reed declared huffily. "I'm not a mind reader, Clyde."

"Okay, everyone," Clyde ordered, taking charge. "It's a crisis, but a small one. Laureen, get ready to redo her face. Reed, then you'll do Kelly's hair over—long and in big, loose curls, right, Vanessa?"

Vanessa gave him a sheepish grin. "Absolutely."

Clyde examined Kelly critically. "You'll be superb," he said, lifting Kelly's hair back and squinting at the effect. "Perfect—a real American beauty rose; just what I wanted."

There was no time for apologies; Kelly was whisked back to the makeup table. "We need pink tones for your lips and eyes," Laureen said briskly, "with a warm mauve for your cheeks and a shimmery highlighter. Here, let's get rid of this color stripe. . . ."

"Paisley," Vanessa barked, "why are you hanging around here? Get into your first costume—there's hardly any time left!"

"Thanks a lot, Kelly," Paisley leaned over to whisper in Kelly's ear, her voice still thick from crying. "You upstaged me again."

Stricken, Kelly tried to rise from her chair to

explain that it had been a mistake, a freak accident—but Paisley was gone, dragged away by Vanessa to be fitted into her first gown.

Kelly wanted to hide. Nothing was going right at all! She had meant to help Paisley, and instead had gotten into an even bigger mess; Paisley would never believe her now.

When Laureen finished with Kelly's face, Reed appeared. "Lift your head," he ordered. "Lucky —this green works fine," he said, combing through the tangled mess of Kelly's hair. "Look— with the pin curls out, it's spread all through one side of your hair, as if we'd frosted your hair in green. I love it—I can really use it—fabulous!"

Deftly, Reed began winding the hair on the right side of Kelly's head around a curling iron, adding ripples to the tinted hair. Kelly was too heartsick to pay much attention. But when Reed hastily put the finishing touches on her hair, loose and flowing into rippling waves, she was conscious of a few envious looks.

"Get to the dresser—hurry!" Reed pushed Kelly toward the runway.

There wasn't a moment to spare. "Oh—wait a minute," Kelly cried. She still had on her jeans and sneakers. "I'll just get into a robe," she said, reaching for one of the plain white wrappers the girls wore in between numbers.

"There's no time."

Reed shoved, and Kelly found herself in the hands of the dressers, Ruby and George. George actually reached down and unzipped Kelly's jeans, slapping away her hands as she tried to do it herself.

"Be a good girl," he ordered, yanking the jeans off before Kelly could say a word.

"Great," Ruby said sarcastically, "ankle socks! Where are your panty hose?"

"I didn't wear them—" Kelly stuttered. She bent and ripped the socks off her feet, before George or Ruby could do it for her. "I meant to change when I got here."

"Forget it." George held out a pair of sleek heels. "Step into these. Fit?"

"They're awfully tight," Kelly said. She jammed her toes into the shoes: her bare feet swelled. Five minutes in these and she'd be crippled for life.

"Fine." George obviously hadn't listened. "Grab some hose on your way out, after your first number, okay? You'll need them; some of your dresses are slit to the waist and we can't have panties showing through."

From the other side of the curtain, Kelly heard Vanessa's voice beginning the introduction to Clyde's "Out of This World" fashion fantasy. Then she heard tinkling bells and strange, eerie sound effects, and realized it was the taped music. Unearthly melodies began to fill the room from the loudspeakers, and in front of her, the first model was sent sliding through the curtains.

A burst of wild applause erupted from the other side, out in the room that was invisible to Kelly. She felt a surge of panic.

"Steady," Ruby urged. "Stay cool—take a deep breath. And get these clothes off!"

Without a word of warning, Ruby reached up and yanked Kelly's T-shirt over her head, leaving her in underpants and bra in front of everyone.

"Holy cow!" George exclaimed. "Who told you to wear that bra?"

Instinctively, Kelly folded her arms across her chest.

"You can't have straps on. You should be wearing a unitard, or nothing," George said.

"Well, she isn't," Ruby answered. "Take the bra off," she ordered Kelly curtly.

Kelly was horrified at the thought of undressing in front of any stranger, and especially a man. Keeping one arm right across her chest, she reached awkwardly behind and unfastened her bra. A lot of good it had done her to wear her silky beige, the bra that models usually wore on jobs because it didn't show through anything. No one told her to wear a strapless tonight, or mentioned that her panties would show either.

She stood still, her bra unhooked, too embarrassed to let it drop to the floor. Finally, she shrugged the shoulder straps down and left the bra pinned against her front, trying to act casual, as if she had forgotten all about it. That way, when they handed her the dress to put on, she could manage to keep herself covered.

Maybe modest girls don't belong in this business, she thought, flooded with doubts. It seemed with every new assignment, she either made a mistake or embarrassed herself. She knew that people sometimes laughed at her, like the time at her first photo session when she made the male hairstylist leave the dressing room before she'd change clothes. Meg and Nina said she'd get used to it, but she still rebelled when she heard people discussing her body as if she were a piece of meat.

"Does Clyde want any bounce in this dress?" George was saying. "I don't want her bouncing if Clyde wants her tight."

"She won't bounce," Ruby argued. "Look at

her—she's small, and there's plenty of muscle tone."

"Then no bra," George declared. Kelly held onto her bra even tighter, knowing she was acting foolish but unable to stop.

"Honey," Ruby laughed, "you're priceless. But stop kidding around now—hold up your arms."

The only thing she could do was turn around. Then Kelly closed her eyes and raised her arms over her head. She felt her bra drop to the floor, and then a dress slid over her body. Kelly flinched: the fabric was icy cold against her skin and she felt goose bumps rise all over. She turned back to face George and Ruby, and they pulled the dress into place, smoothing the wrinkles and rumples quickly and surely, paying no attention to the body underneath the tightly fitted fabric. *Just wait until Jennifer hears about this!* Kelly thought.

George set a feathered headdress onto her head, anchoring it quickly with a couple of hairpins; Kelly was sure the headdress would go flying off with the first step she took. Meanwhile, she listened to Vanessa's commentary, straining to catch any mention of her own name. She thought she had plenty of time left to fix her headdress and adjust the dress, which was pulling under the right armhole and driving her crazy with a need to scratch.

But without warning, Kelly felt herself pushed from behind through those forbidding curtains and she was out front, on the runway.

Flashbulbs exploded in her eyes. She froze, stunned and not knowing where to go or what to do.

"Move!" someone hissed, and blindly, Kelly began walking straight ahead down the runway.

At first there was silence—Kelly understood what people meant when they said time stood still: she had an eerie sensation of being in a void—alone in the universe, unable to see or hear or think clearly. Vaguely, she heard her name mentioned and realized it was Vanessa, announcing her appearance to the hushed audience:

"Kelly, our own Earth Maiden, in a very down-to-earth offering: luminescent iced-green satin, touched with wisps of cloudy white chiffon. For memorable evenings on earth!"

Numbly, Kelly was aware of wild applause and appreciative murmurs circulating through the room, and she realized she was moving down the runway. She felt immense relief. *Thank goodness I didn't remain frozen like a dummy! Paisley's training yesterday really paid off.* She hoped she was moving in time to the music; she hadn't been paying any attention at all.

Her eyes were focused somewhere near the ceiling of the wall at the back of the room, as Paisley had suggested. But now that her nerves were steadier, she couldn't resist lowering her gaze to the audience. There were so many people, all looking straight at her. For a moment she felt faint. What if she tripped and fell flat on her face? No one would ever hire her again, and it would be in all the newspapers and kids at school would make fun of her forever! She swallowed deeply, trying not to pay attention to the faces at all.

She barely recognized the transformed Star-light Roof. A hundred round tables, each draped in a shimmering pastel tablecloth, filled the floor.

The different colors caught the light from an overhead spotlight, and sparkled like thousands of multicolored stars. Exotic flowers and feathers were suspended in a net that hung from the ceiling, and stars and planets were scattered among them. Everything was bathed in a soft light that made the women beautiful and the men handsome: it was all magical, unreal. Kelly's fear was forgotten now; she only wished she had time to stand and gaze at the scene.

But she was at the end of the runway: should she turn and go back immediately, or should she spin a few times, as Paisley had shown her the day before? She heard Vasessa begin another description, and decided she had best get out of the way of the next girl.

Turning sharply, Kelly started back up the runway—too late! Six models, three on each side, were prancing toward her—there was no room for her, unless she headed straight up the middle of the runway. With no other choice, she strode quickly toward the curtain.

"Stay there!" she heard someone hiss. It was Paisley, to Kelly's left, raising her eyebrows frantically, trying to signal Kelly not to leave the runway. "You're the star," Paisley hissed, trying to talk without moving her lips, "the end, the end!"

Suddenly Kelly realized what Paisley was trying to say to her. As the earth girl, Kelly was supposed to be the center of attention; literally center stage. She was supposed to stay at the end of the runway, surrounded by the blond and redheaded Star Children, contrasting to their brilliant colors with her pale green dress, her dark hair.

But she was facing the wrong way—headed straight for the curtain and the dressing area! She had to cover her mistake, and what's more, she had to make it back to the end of the runway before Vanessa ended her commentary. There was only one way out. When you were in a jam, you had to make your mistake look as if done on purpose. There was no time to be subtle. Just like in a track meet, Kelly had to make it to the finish line.

Flinging her arms out in what she hoped was a graceful theatrical move (and not a muscle-bound, athletic gesture), Kelly whirled around once, intending to do her version of an earth maiden leaping for joy—right to the end of the runway. But as she turned, her outstretched arms knocked into Adrianne, and both girls momentarily lost their balance. There was an audible gasp from the audience; this was hardly the dreamy, lighter-than-air effect Kelly had hoped for.

She looked straight at the audience and giggled, flashing a brilliant smile. It worked: the audience laughed in response, breaking the tension, and Kelly's blazing smile was genuine as they applauded her antics. She continued smiling and laughing as she strode toward the runway's end, as if it were all part of how an earth maiden behaved.

The applause was wonderful: they loved her! Kelly caught Paisley's eye as she did one last turn. As Vanessa said, "Thank you, Kelly, and our Star Children," Kelly winked, and this time she bounded up the runway with real joy. She had done it! She had run into trouble but had used her head and her personality to turn a potential disaster into a small triumph.

She was beaming with relief as she came through the curtains, but there was no time to savor her success.

"Smart girl," Ruby said as she yanked the stunning dress over Kelly's head. That was the sum total of the praise Kelly received.

Disappointment overwhelmed her. No way could she savor anything—not even the magical dress. Her moment of stardom was instantly forgotten as George and Ruby whisked the dress onto a hanger, paying more attention to it than to her.

"Here, kid, catch." Ruby tossed her panty hose and a flesh-colored bandeau bra, one that wouldn't show in the revealing dresses. Kelly put the lingerie on with relief, ignoring Ruby and George's amused looks. So she was modest; she couldn't help it. Maybe someday she wouldn't mind the locker room aspects of her profession, but right now she was glad to be decently covered and protected from prying eyes.

There was no time to spare, however: she was immediately thrust into another dress.

"My feet hurt," she complained. "Isn't there another pair of shoes, size nine?"

But no one paid any attention; the last thing anyone cared about was Kelly's feet. Meanwhile, Reed was calling her name.

"Adjustment, adjustment," he yelled.

Although she had no idea what he meant she hurried to his table.

"Gotta pick this hair up," he said through a mouthful of hairpins. "Show the neck of that dress."

Kelly's next outfit was a multilayered chiffon that fastened with a high collar: she hadn't even seen it as it had been pulled over her head, and her glance at the brilliant red fabric in Reed's mirror was something of a shock. The dress had been artfully constructed without shoulders or sides, yet somehow, it clung to her body, outlining every curve. Only by staring intently did she finally see the dress was held together by transparent net fabric, giving an illusion of absolute nudity. The shredded layers of red cloth were sewn separately to this netting, and each layer moved as she bent forward, revealing the slightly iridescent, filmy net fabric underneath. The effect was of a beautiful nude body covered with flower petals. The dress was so flattering and so beautiful, Kelly couldn't feel the least bit of embarrassment at its bareness. *Maybe I'm getting used to this business after all*, she thought as Reed rearranged her hair.

She wondered if the models ever got a really good idea of what they looked like. There wasn't any time to admire yourself in a mirror before your cue. There was barely time to pin and tuck those dresses that didn't lie right on a particular girl. One model whose side seam had split as the dress was pulled over her head had to endure the walk down the runway with a dozen pins jabbing into her side. Later, when the poor girl undressed again, Kelly saw the line of tiny red dots where the pins had stuck. The model never said a word: she didn't have time to notice the pain.

Changes were instantaneous and complaints worthless. You had to grin and bear it, Kelly was learning.

"Ouch!" She grabbed at her head.

"Sorry," Reed managed. He had finished. Kelly caught a quick glimpse as she hurried back to the dressers; Reed had lifted just the hair around her face, mindful of Clyde's instructions to let Kelly's long, full hair contrast to the short hair of the other models.

Kelly was determined to pay more attention to what was going on around her. She didn't want any false steps this time—no more runway collisions.

To her surprise, she noticed an assistant standing by the curtains who cued her with a pointed finger when it was her turn on the runway. *No wonder someone pushed me the last time,* she thought. *I hadn't even noticed that woman!*

The audience reacted with pleasure as Kelly sailed through the curtains, the petals of her dress lifting and moving in the breeze she created with her bouncy stride. This time, she paced herself to the music, and it was fun, showing off the beauty of the incredible dress as people murmured and clapped in admiration. She had time for several spins at the end of the runway, and remembering her moment of panic last time, she promised herself not to look straight at the audience. But people seemed to have different expections of their Earth Maiden; she heard them calling to her, until finally she scanned the audience, smiling and making quick eye contact with the crowd. They kept on clapping and calling until she felt she had no choice but to do a quick earth-maiden sprint up the runway and back. The audience went wild, laughing and applauding, and she knew her prancing was flattering to the fluttery dress; but what would Vanessa think of her stealing extra runway time?

Anxiously, she scanned Vanessa's face, but all she saw was a knowing smile, as if Vanessa had expected Kelly to steal the show. The *ooh's* and *ah's* continued, so Kelly gave another spin or two, but finally Vanessa gave a curt nod and Kelly knew it was a signal to head for the curtains. She flashed the audience a last impish smile and threw in a couple of dramatic spins as she burst back into the dressing area.

"Are you *sure* this is your first live show?" Ruby eyed her skeptically. "You're a real scene-stealer."

"It's my first," Kelly said gaily. She did seem to have a natural flair for this work after all. Meg would be so proud of her—and wait until she told her friends what a smashing success Earth Maiden had been. *My friends; does that include Jennifer or not?* She frowned. *If Eric could see me now, the audience eating out of my hand, maybe he'd realize other people find me desirable, and then he'd want me for himself.*

Ruby and George, removing the petal dress and fitting the next one over her head, noticed her expression.

"Don't worry, honey," Ruby assured her, "it won't be too much longer. Just ignore those aching feet."

"It isn't my feet," Kelly said; she had forgotten all about the too tight shoes. She was frowning because of Eric; it had been a mistake to think of him. All of a sudden, the fashion show seemed less glamorous, her appearance less important. Eric was home, alone with Jennifer, and Kelly Blake was the last thing they'd be thinking about.

"You're a big hit," Ruby said. "Clyde will

notice, don't worry about that. You'll get lots more runway work."

"I'm not sure I want more," Kelly answered.

"If you believe that, you're dumber than me."

The three of them looked up to see Paisley, casual in her beige bodysuit, coolly staring at Kelly. "You *are* a surprise, Kelly, honey. Taking over the whole show, single-handedly."

Kelly groaned. "Would you leave me alone? I nearly fell over Adrianne, didn't you see? The rest was just to cover up my mistakes."

"Yesterday she was begging me for help," Paisley continued, ignoring Kelly's remark. "And today she steals my thunder. Watch out for her, George—she'll use you, too."

With that parting remark, Paisley stomped away to get her makeup freshened.

"It's not true," Kelly protested.

"Save it," Ruby snapped. "Lift your arms . . ."

Kelly sighed. "I know—and hurry. There's no time for complaining." The petal dress came off and another—an innocent creation of pale pink fabric—slid over her head.

Nine

"This is the big finale," Ruby told Kelly as she pulled her final change for the evening over Kelly's head. "You have some time before you go on again. Better get your hair and makeup retouched."

Dutifully, Kelly waited at the makeup table while Laureen worked on another model. Kelly's shoes really *did* hurt her, and she leaned down to tug them off her feet.

"Don't," Laureen warned. "Your feet have swelled by now; if you take those shoes off, you'll never get them back on." She finished her other model and motioned for Kelly to sit in front of the brightly lit mirror. As Laureen appraised her costume, Kelly realized she had barely noted this new outfit.

"Those deep purples and reds are kind of dramatic next to your pale skin," Laureen murmured. "Let's contrast it even more. I'm going to apply some near-white foundation and powder, the kind Japanese actors use on stage. It's usually a real fantasy look, but I'll quiet it down with some blue tones. That will make it more natural looking, without making you look ordinary."

"Blue?" Kelly said vaguely. The color of her skin tone was the last thing on her mind. Now that she had time to sit, her feet ached unbearably, and the high-collared dress scratched her throat.

"I'm not crazy," Laureen continued, "brunettes like you have blue undertones to their skin. You'll see—it won't look anything like it sounds."

"I believe you." Halfheartedly, she watched Laureen apply the dramatic makeup.

"Now for your eyes, something spectacular." Laureen created a fantasy mask over Kelly's eyes and eyebrows, repeating the same mauves and reds of the dress and adding an iridescent coppery gold around the edges, to make her eyes shimmer and shine. Kelly stared at herself in the mirror. The everyday Kelly Blake was gone, replaced by a mysterious stranger—a creature from another planet who'd never heard of friends who misjudged her, or had crushes on boys who didn't like her. In a way, it was a relief not to feel like a regular human being with regular problems. Still, Kelly frowned at the makeup.

"It's not very 'earth maiden,' is it?" she said doubtfully.

"Sure it is," Laureen insisted. "Don't be too literal, now. Clyde wants a very dramatic effect for the ending." She stepped back to admire her work, adding another coat of lip gloss to deepen Kelly's red lips. "Perfect," Laureen announced.

"Now get your hair done—be careful! Don't twist your neck. You'll get makeup all over that collar and ruin it!"

Kelly pulled at the tight collar. "But it's itching like crazy."

"Don't touch that—and no scratching," Laureen scolded. "That dress is a lot harder to replace than you are, and I don't have time to do your makeup over. So hands off."

"I wish someone around here would treat me like a person," Kelly sulked.

"Oh, don't get on your high horse," Laureen said. "What did you expect?"

"Someone's in a bad mood," Reed said when Kelly sat at his makeup mirror. He lifted her head to get a better look at her hairdo. "What's the matter with you? You were floating on air a minute ago."

Kelly shrugged. There was no way she could explain her mood to Reed. "I guess I got too excited before, and now I feel let down."

"I've seen that happen," Reed said. "But you have to pretend you're feeling cheerful and peppy. That's what people forget about this work; it isn't as easy as it seems."

He sighed at her makeup job. "Laureen didn't give me much chance," he told Kelly. "Your face is so spectacular, no one's going to notice my hair." Nevertheless, he went to work, teasing and spraying and lifting Kelly's hair all around her face in a windblown halo of rippling waves. He sent her on her way with an encouraging pat on the back. "Knock 'em dead, sweetheart."

George had a surprise in store for her: an enormous headdress to wear with this final outfit.

He nestled it over her forehead, crushing down the hairdo Reed had just labored over, pinning it into place with sharp little stabs.

"Sorry," he told Kelly. "Hard to tell where your scalp is with all this hair."

The headdress was stunning, but it threatened to fall over Kelly's forehead onto her face, and George had to rig up a system of thin black wires to hold it in place.

"Gorgeous," he pronounced, and Ruby nodded in agreement. "Clyde will adore it," she said.

Kelly walked to the nearest mirror. The headpiece looked like a coppery-gold starburst, with velvet and satin ribbons bunched over each ear, falling into long streamers down past her shoulders. Her hair cascaded in ripples over her back.

The effect was indescribable. Her dress, of a silky material Kelly had never seen before, had long panels instead of sleeves: they fastened at the shoulders and wrists, but caught the breeze to billow and flutter when she moved. Again, she had on a sort of transparent underdress, and the patterned skirt fell from the bodice, clinging to her body but floating about her as she moved. The skirt ended slightly above the ankles in front and came to a point in back, fluttering around her heels.

"It's magnificent," Ruby said, admiring her.

"But every time I take a step the material catches on my shoes." Kelly did a practice turn and the fabric wrapped around her ankles, nearly tripping her.

"I can't walk in this," she said crankily, "I'll fall flat on my face." This was all she needed—not only was she in a sudden bad mood, exhausted and unable to stop thinking about Jennifer alone with Eric, but she was bound to make a fool of herself and ruin the entire fashion show.

The other girls brushed by, on their way to their final walk down the runway.

"Look what escaped from the zoo," Paisley whispered as she passed. She elbowed Adrianne, who looked at Kelly's painted mask and giggled nastily. "Monkey face," Paisley sang, "you've got the cutest little monkey face . . ."

Kelly flushed; tears threatened to fill her eyes. Ruby and George fussed over her, assuring her that she looked "fabulous" and "absolutely incredible," but all Kelly knew was that her feet were bleeding, her neck was scratched raw by the miserable collar, and her head was aching from the wires George had wound around it. The dress kept snagging on her shoes, the headdress was slipping down her forehead, and at that moment she had no doubt she looked as ridiculous as Paisley said: a monkey escaped from the zoo.

"Go—go," George hissed. She had missed her cue, and as she stumbled to the curtains she again felt herself pushed from behind. She had had enough; all she wanted to do was run home and sink into a warm bath. But there was no escape. Gallantly, she sailed down the runway, holding her head high.

The audience will sense the change in my mood, she thought. No doubt they would be disappointed, but she couldn't keep a smile on her face. No matter how hard she tried, the Earth Maiden was gone. She felt like a little kid, cranky and tired and on the verge of miserable tears— how had she fooled herself into thinking she was some glamorous creature?

When she reached the end of the runway she

hesitated; for some reason people were applauding, and the music showed no change in volume or tempo. Twirling once, she caught Vanessa's eye and Vanessa gave her an encouraging nod as if to say keep moving. Halfheartedly, Kelly twirled a few times as she made her way up the runway toward the curtains, praying for each turn to be her last. But again Vanessa nodded to her—keep moving.

There was more commentary; a summary of all the clothes that had been shown that evening, as each model reappeared, some more than once, to reshow a gown. *Vanessa's descriptions are almost embarrassing*, Kelly thought, listening to herself being described in the most flowery terms:

". . . and our fiery Earth Maiden, Kelly—sultry and provocative, truly a temptress in Clyde's finest creation of sensual earthiness . . ."

When the house lights dimmed, Kelly felt immense relief. *Get these shoes off me*, she felt like screaming. On either side of her, the models headed for the curtains while the applause and appreciative murmurs continued. Kelly waited a moment for the last couple of girls to turn, and then she began to follow them back. But someone leaped onto the runway beside her, holding her firmly in place.

The house lights came up, and there was thunderous applause. Kelly was standing next to Clyde Mason himself.

"You were perfect," he said quietly, "super—great instincts; a real showgirl. Super job."

Vanessa introduced Clyde, and Kelly glanced at him sideways. *He must have planned this moment*, she realized; his velvet suit and her silk dress looked dramatic together.

Clyde stepped back. Holding out Kelly's arm, he gestured for her to curtsy. The last time Kelly curtsied she was in third grade. Her dancing school teacher had thought all boys should know how to bow, and all girls should know how to curtsy. It was how you greeted royalty, the teacher had explained. Everyone thought the teacher was crazy—when would royalty ever come to New Jersey?

But to Kelly, Clyde Mason seemed like royalty, and she did the best curtsy she could manage. Really, it *was* thrilling to be alone with Clyde Mason, the famous designer, while people applauded and a few even whistled. Finally, Clyde bent and gave her a quick kiss, smiled at her radiantly, and walked her through one last turn. Kelly's pain and fatigue were forgotten now. With a little push, Clyde aimed her at the curtains, and Kelly took her final walk up the runway. She couldn't resist one last spin before disappearing through the curtain.

What an exit! But if she expected applause and admiration, she was sadly mistaken. It was pure chaos backstage; girls ran around in various stages of undress, flinging dresses and shoes and accessories wherever they felt like flinging them. Laureen was packing up her makeup equipment, and Reed was chasing after girls who still had his clips and combs in their hair.

There was the kind of high-spirited teasing and joking that always follows enormous tension. *They're all as relieved as I am that it's over*, Kelly thought. The first thing she did was to take off the horrible shoes, which by now were plastered to her swollen feet, and peel off her panty hose.

She groaned at the sight of the huge raw spots on each of her heels. "Band-Aids," she gasped, grabbing Laureen's shoulder and pointing at her feet.

"Somewhere around here," Laureen said. "Try over there." She pointed to a storage room set back from the dressing area, and Kelly hobbled over in her bare feet, carefully avoiding the hair clips and straight pins that littered the floor. She walked straight into Paisley Gregg.

"If it isn't Miss Prima Donna," Paisley sneered. "Well, congratulations—everyone thinks you're brilliant. You really know how to get attention."

"Shut up, Paisley," Kelly groaned, shuffling inside the storage room and plopping down on a cardboard box. "I don't want to fight. Think what you want about me—all I care about is my feet."

Paisley had followed her inside. "Don't tell me to shut up—you think you're so special . . ."

Kelly exploded, all her patience gone. "Look, Paisley—let's get this straight. I didn't try to get all the attention, not today and not yesterday. I couldn't care less about impressing Metzy Metzenberg, and it really ticks me off that you accused me of doing something I had no intention of doing, and didn't even give me a chance to defend myself. That stinks."

"Poor baby," Paisley said.

Kelly ignored the sarcastic tone; she had to get everything out in the open. "Whether you believe me or not, you're the one who should apologize—needling me, calling me names on the runway; that really threw me."

Paisley was genuinely surprised. "It did? I didn't think anything would bother you."

"Then why did you do it?"

"To get even. You're spoiled, and *that* stinks."

Kelly laughed out loud. "Me? Spoiled? You should spend a day with my family to see how *spoiled* I am—I'm no pampered rich kid, if that's what you think. No one ever gave me anything I didn't earn . . ."

Paisley hooted. "You're either a liar or stupider than I thought. Meg Dorian has given you everything from day one."

"What are you talking about?" Kelly peered up at her from beneath the headdress. It had slipped even further, and she had to hold it up with one hand to keep it out of her eyes.

Paisley was incredulous. "This may come as a shock, honey, but you haven't done one ordinary thing since the day you became a model."

Kelly eyed her, a puzzled look on her face. "I have too . . ."

"No, dear," Paisley said haughtily, in the tone of voice that infuriated Kelly. "An ordinary model works months, even years, to get where you are. How about a go-see—an appointment to look you over and see if you're right for a particular job— how about a go-see every half hour of the day, every day, dragging your portfolio all over town, smiling like a fool while they tell you you're too tall or too short or too plain or too pretty, too smart looking, too dumb looking, too wholesome, not wholesome enough. Did you ever do that?"

"No," Kelly slowly admitted. "But I never asked for special treatment . . ."

Paisley laughed out loud. "Ask? Meg is so excited about you, she spared you all the pain.

Don't be dumb—do you think every girl does magazine covers her first week on the job? Meg is treating you like a queen, and you don't even know it! What a dope!"

Kelly squirmed. "Knock it off, Paisley—I'm not stupid. I just didn't realize what Meg has done for me."

"I'll say you didn't."

With a shock, Kelly realized Paisley was jealous. Why hadn't she realized it before? No wonder Paisley got so angry whenever Kelly was noticed; if Kelly had had to go through the things Paisley described, she would probably be jealous or angry, too, about a girl who'd had it easy. Suddenly Kelly felt much better.

"Wait a minute—I think I know why you flipped out yesterday, when I got so much attention," she said.

"That didn't bother me half as much as what you did today."

"Today? What . . ."

"With Clyde. I finally got him to look at my sketches, and then you barged in and suddenly all anyone could talk about was you, Earth Maiden. Fussing over you, the big star of the evening."

"That's not my fault. I didn't have any control over that—I can't apologize for being a brunette."

Paisley made an impatient face. "You always have an excuse," she said.

"Stop it," Kelly ordered angrily. "Give me a break! Just shut up or I'll, I'll—" She tugged at the heavy headpiece. "I'll make you eat this ridiculous thing!" She gave a harsh tug and painfully pulled out a handful of her hair. She let out a frustrated scream. "Get this thing off me!"

"Don't pull at it," Paisley scolded. "You'll only make it worse." To Kelly's surprise, Paisley reached over and tried unwrapping the wires. "What a mess," she said. "You're stuck in this—forget it."

Suddenly, Kelly began to giggle. "Clyde should see me now—what would he think of *this* earth maiden?" Kelly laughed, unable to stop for a while, and although Paisley didn't join in, Kelly thought she detected a smile playing around her lips.

"I mean it, Paisley," Kelly said when she stopped laughing. "I didn't try to upstage you or anyone, really I didn't."

"Maybe you didn't plan it but you sure made a big impression."

"It was exciting," Kelly admitted. "I really loved it—though if you hadn't helped me yesterday I would have blown it."

Paisley stared, startled. "You mean it?"

"Sure I mean it," Kelly said, peeking from under the headdress.

"Well," Paisley said slowly, "to tell you the truth, it *was* a bad time to show Clyde my drawings. Anyway, I guess it wasn't your fault he hated them."

"He didn't hate them," Kelly protested. "He couldn't—they were wonderful."

"You really think so?" Paisley peered at her suspiciously.

"Honest—they were terrific. You should keep at it; you're really talented. I can't draw a straight line."

Paisley tried to hide her feelings, but Kelly could see how pleased she was at the compliment. "I was always good at drawing," Paisley said.

She looked at Kelly thoughtfully. "You know, you looked good tonight; not like you escaped from a zoo. But you should have seen your face when I said that—you turned bright red!" Paisley giggled, and Kelly knew some kind of truce had been reached.

Together, they untangled the rest of the wires from Kelly's hair and Paisley lifted the horrible headdress away as Kelly rubbed her sore forehead.

"If I was red it was because of this headdress," Kelly complained. "It kept slipping and I was terrified I would trip and fall flat on my face. And this makeup! I do look like a monkey, with this stuff all around my eyes!"

"But everyone raved about you," Paisley said. "They said you looked unearthly—distracted and romantic."

"Romantic!" Kelly shrieked with laughter. "I never wanted to get something over with so much in my life! That distracted look was me thinking about my feet, and my best friend, at home with my boyfriend . . ." She stopped herself. It was decent of Paisley to apologize, but Kelly hadn't meant to tell her life story.

"What about your boyfriend?" Paisley said immediately.

"He isn't even really my boyfriend," Kelly said, feeling herself flush, "just someone I kind of like . . ."

"Don't tell me you have boy problems!" Paisley shrieked in delight.

"Don't look so pleased."

"So you're not perfect." Paisley grinned.

"Me—perfect?" Kelly debated whether she

should admit how inferior Paisley always made her feel. "No one's perfect," she said instead.

Paisley sat down on a cardboard box opposite Kelly, stretching and clasping her arms behind her back. "Well, well—so Kelly Blake is human after all. Welcome to the club."

"Yesterday I wondered if *you* were human," Kelly said. "I could have killed you when I found out your age—seventeen and only modeling a year longer than me. What an act you put on!"

Paisley shrugged. "A year is a long time."

"Long enough to get your act down," Kelly said. "You seemed perfect."

"I know," Paisley said. "I try to be. It's this business—you know, don't let anyone know you're scared or hurt when they reject you . . ."

They were both silent for a minute.

"Paisley," Kelly finally said, "it helps to know you feel that way, too. It *is* hard sometimes."

Paisley gave her a grudging look of admiration. "Even if it was a mistake, you did that first number perfectly. The last one, too."

"Just find me a Band-Aid," Kelly said. "My poor feet will never be the same."

As Kelly bandaged her feet, Paisley watched her thoughtfully. "Kelly, will you do me a big favor?"

"Sure," Kelly said brightly. She couldn't help feeling terrific now that she and Paisley had made up.

"Will you use your influence to make Von Metzenberg look at my sketches?"

Kelly's mouth dropped. "Influence—I met him once!"

Paisley pouted, and Kelly sighed. "Paisley, I promise—if I ever see Mr. Von Metzenberg again, I'll mention your dress designs."

Paisley's face lit up and she grabbed Kelly in a big hug. "I knew I could count on you," she cried. "Von Metzenberg knows lots of rich and important people. He could introduce me to society women, and they'd order my dresses, and he could lend me the money to get started—it would be fantastic!" Almost waltzing across the room, Paisley opened the supply room door and went outside.

Kelly was exhausted, physically and mentally. She stretched and gave a good, hearty yawn. It was time for Cinderella to go home. She picked up the hem of her gown and, balancing on her toes, did one last swirling turn. Then she followed Paisley out into the dressing area.

Ten

"Where is everybody?" Kelly stared at the empty dressing area. It was a shambles; scraps of paper, hairpins, torn panty hose, empty lipstick cases, and other things were scattered over the floor. But there wasn't a person in sight.

"The other girls all went home, I guess," Paisley said with a distracted look on her face. "No reason to stick around."

"But where are all Clyde's assistants?"

"I don't know—they must be around here someplace."

"Well, let's get these dresses off." Kelly reached behind her, struggling to unfasten the high neck of her dress. "Paisley, give me a hand— I can't get this undone."

"Huh? Oh, sure . . ." Paisley stood behind Kelly, prying at the too-tight hook and eye.

"Kelly," she said thoughtfully, "we worked pretty hard tonight, don't you think?"

"I'll say," Kelly replied. "It was fun, but I'm glad it's over."

"Me, too."

"Haven't you got that unhooked yet?"

"Huh? Oh, yeah, nearly." Paisley was silent for a moment. "Boy, Kelly, I'm really beat after all that hard work, and we can't even enjoy the ball. It hardly seems fair."

Kelly sighed. "It *is* a kind of letdown—putting on jeans and sneakers after wearing all these glamorous clothes all night."

"Don't you wish you could wear gowns like this for real," Paisley said, "and dance all night, and drink champagne . . . ?"

"I don't like champagne," Kelly admitted, laughing, "but dancing all night in the arms of someone new—that sounds really appealing."

"You really *do* have boyfriend trouble," Paisley said.

"I told you, I don't have a boyfriend."

"Oh, honey, don't sound so down. You deserve better tonight. You deserve to be pampered, to enjoy yourself . . . After all, if Clyde Mason sells his dresses, it's all thanks to you—you made his dresses look good."

"That's true, I guess," Kelly said.

"No doubt about it. In fact, if the Children's Fund makes tons of money tonight, that's also because of you, and me. We put on a great show and helped a very worthy cause. You're right, Kelly—we deserve some thanks."

"I didn't say that," Kelly protested, still pulling at the stubborn collar.

"But we're the ones who should be out there,

dancing the night away. Wouldn't you love it? That great music, going to waste!"

"We'd look pretty funny, dancing in our jeans. There—I got it." Kelly unhooked the dress and began to pull it off.

"Don't take the dress off—wait a minute."

"For what?"

"For what?" Paisley laughed, acting as if Kelly had made a joke. "We can't wear our jeans to the ball, you said so yourself. We'd better wear these dresses."

"To the ball—are you crazy?" Kelly yelled. "I never said . . ."

"But you agree it makes perfect sense." Paisley jumped right in, pleading her case skillfully. "We deserve it, you said so yourself. They owe us a little pleasure after all the hard work we did for them. And what harm could it do?"

"None—but we're not invited," Kelly said.

"No, but we could just take a look—we won't stay. Think of all those celebrities out there, in the flesh."

Kelly thought of them; she also thought of Eric and Jennifer together, laughing and having fun. It wasn't fair. Why should some society ladies have all the fun, when Kelly was the one who had done all the work?

"Vanessa told us to put these dresses on the rack when we were through," Kelly said. "They have to go back to Clyde's showroom tonight. Don't forget, these are exclusive designs—she was very firm about that."

"No one's going to steal Clyde's designs now," Paisley said. "They've been photographed—they're not secret any more."

"But still," Kelly insisted, "Vanessa said the dresses have to go back tonight."

Paisley tapped her foot impatiently. "Do you see Vanessa? Is she around anywhere?"

"Not right in this room, but she must be here someplace."

"Sure—she and Clyde's other assistants are somewhere in the hotel having a celebration drink. They always do that after a show; they don't go home and go to bed. She'll take the dresses back later. Why should we be the only ones who don't have any fun? Is that fair?"

Kelly laughed. "I was thinking the exact same thing," she admitted. "I don't think it's right; we do all the work and then we're sent home like children."

Just a few minutes ago, Clyde Mason himself was praising her good instincts. Now Kelly's instincts told her to attend the ball. *Even Cinderella attended the ball*, she told herself.

Plus, her mother would be waiting up for her tonight, eager to hear how her favorite movie stars looked in real life. No one would believe that she had been this close to all those famous people and just went home; only a fool would do that. What harm was there in taking a little peek inside?

"We'll just take a look," Kelly said. "We won't stay, but we'll at least see the ball." Now that the decision was made, she was excited. *Wait until I tell everyone at school about the ball!*

"And then we'll come right back and put these dresses away," she continued. "I feel funny, wearing them without permission."

"Then put your shoes on and let's go, quick— Vanessa could get back any second," Paisley said.

"Shoes—oh, no," Kelly wailed. "I'll never get those back on these feet. What'll I do? I can't go out there barefoot."

"I know!" Paisley hunted around the debris in the dressing room, came up with her bag, and pulled out a pair of black Chinese slippers. "These are my emergency shoes. I always take them in my bag in case I need them in between shots, or if my shoes won't show in a photo. Uncomfortable shoes can ruin a day's work."

"Tell me about it." Gratefully, Kelly slipped the shoes onto her feet. They fit fine; just tight enough to stay on, but not so tight they pressed against her bandaged heels. "They'll do for now. Anyway, no one's really going to see us."

"Come on, hurry."

"Wait, my face—I can't leave this makeup on, not if we don't want to attract attention."

"All right, but make it quick!"

Kelly scrubbed at the extravagant makeup with tissues and then quickly dragged a brush through her hair, which was still outrageous looking, with streaks of color in it. With luck, though, no one at the ball would notice or make a fuss over her.

She could hardly wait to get outside. Paisley was right—it would have been terrible to go home. You couldn't play it safe all your life. Just as long as it wasn't *too* late when she got to the bus station . . .

Paisley pulled her to the curtains leading to the ballroom.

"We can't go out that way," Kelly cried. "Everyone will see us!"

"Don't be a dope! The runway's gone now. Take a look."

Cautiously, Kelly parted the curtains and peered through. The ramp and runway had been taken away, and a bandstand had been set up in its place; Kelly was standing to the side of the orchestra, hidden by some potted plants.

"You're right," she whispered to Paisley. "We'll be pretty well hidden if we stay right behind those plants." She shivered in excitement. "I think I see that actor from television, you know, the one who does the adventure series with the talking car . . ."

"He's great looking," Paisley exclaimed, standing beside Kelly at the curtains. "Let's get closer."

"Just a little," Kelly said. But it was difficult to see everything with the gigantic plants in the way.

Paisley looked at Kelly. "If we stick to the sides of the room, we won't interfere with anyone," she said. After a moment, Kelly nodded her agreement.

Not that people were looking their way. With the runway gone, dancers crowded the dance floor. Along two sides of the room stretched a long buffet table loaded with food; people balanced plates piled high, or roamed from table to table to speak to friends.

Kelly and Paisley drifted out from behind the curtains; no one took any notice.

"I'm glad I got that headdress off," Kelly whispered. "I don't want anyone to spot us."

"They won't. And you're much shorter without heels on," Paisley noted. "No one will recognize you, believe me."

"Look," Kelly cried suddenly, pointing out at the hallway. "There's Vanessa." Surrounded by a group talking animatedly, Vanessa was busy sipping champagne. A waiter hovered nearby with a tray of glasses, and Vanessa emptied one glass and took another from the tray, laughing loudly at someone's joke.

"She won't leave for hours," Paisley said. "We've got plenty of time."

"Just a few more minutes," Kelly agreed, "and then we'll take the dresses back and . . ."

"There he is!" Paisley tugged at Kelly's arm, pulling her toward the crowded dance floor.

"Who?" Kelly craned her neck, searching for the exciting celebrity Paisley had spotted.

"Von Metzenberg!" Paisley started to head straight into the crowd of dancers, but Kelly held her back.

"Von Metzenberg," she echoed in disbelief, "who cares about him? Besides, you can't go out there, we're not supposed to be here—remember?"

"*I* care about him," Paisley said. "Let me go, Kelly."

Kelly eyed Paisley suspiciously. "You don't care about celebrities, do you? You just wanted to corner that poor old man and talk to him about your dress designs. You tricked me."

"Please, Kelly, this is important," Paisley begged. "He adores you; just get him to talk to me, let him get to know me. Then maybe he'll make a business appointment with me. I don't stand a chance otherwise, and you owe it to me; you said so yourself. Didn't I stay and help you learn runway techniques? I helped you in your hour of need."

"But not here, not now," Kelly sputtered. "What if we get caught?"

"Who's going to catch us? Vanessa's busy having fun, and besides, he wouldn't let anyone so much as scold you. Come on, Kelly, he'll protect us, you know it."

Kelly felt herself weakening. It wouldn't do any harm to say hello, and Paisley had a point; adults had a way of ignoring teenagers, even when they had something valuable to say. Paisley's sketches were good; they deserved to be seen by the right people. If spending a few minutes chatting with Von Metzenberg would help Paisley's career, it would be worth the risk of being caught.

Paisley watched her closely. "Unless, of course, you're in a hurry to get back home tonight. Maybe you have other plans . . ."

Again, Kelly pictured Eric and Jennifer, cozy and laughing together, glad to be rid of Kelly.

"Okay, Paisley," she said, "let's go."

Paisley was radiant. "You're a doll," she cried, squeezing Kelly in a big hug. "I won't ever forget this favor—I promise."

"Just hurry," Kelly said grimly. She led the way across the dance floor and between the crowded tables.

Herbert Von Metzenberg was eating busily, ignoring the chatter of the people at his table, and for a moment Kelly lost her nerve. What if he didn't remember her from yesterday? Or what if he recognized the dresses as Clyde's and had them arrested or something?

"Kelly, isn't it?" Von Metzenberg had discovered her, leaping to his feet and extending a hand. "Have a seat. You looked ravishing, my dear, just ravishing. Have you eaten anything, are you hungry?"

"No," Kelly faltered. "I wanted to ask you . . ."

Von Metzenberg barked at one of the men at his table, "Frank—get the girls something to eat."

Frank rose obediently and trotted to the buffet. Paisley seemed impressed, but Von Metzenberg's high-handed manner made Kelly slightly uncomfortable.

"Sit, sit," he told them both, pulling over empty chairs from the nearest table.

"Thank you." Kelly sat primly. "Mr. Von Metzenberg, I was wondering if you remember my friend, Paisley Gregg . . ."

"Another young beauty." Von Metzenberg half smiled.

"Thank you," Paisley simpered. She reached over and took Von Metzenberg's hand. "Won't you dance with me, Metzy?" she said boldly.

Kelly was shocked; no one talked to Von Metzenberg that way, she was sure. Von Metzenberg would have a fit!

But instead, he stroked Paisley's hand, grinning hungrily, as if Paisley were his next course. "Of course," he answered, "but we can't leave Kelly sitting here alone . . ."

"Excuse me—I'd be glad to dance with Kelly."

Alex Hawkins! He appeared at Kelly's side, tall and even more handsome than Kelly remembered. The elegant tuxedo brought out his good looks, contrasting with his blond hair and sparkling eyes. She felt a peculiar rushing in her stomach that left her slightly breathless.

"Alex," she managed to say, "I didn't know you'd be here."

"Wasn't supposed to be," he said quickly,

pulling Kelly to her feet. He bowed slightly to Von Metzenberg. "Excuse us, please." He led Kelly onto the dance floor. "Rescue mission completed," he said.

"Rescue? I don't understand."

"Metzy eats young girls alive," Alex told her, but with a teasing look in his eyes. "Paisley is more his speed. Anyway, I wanted to be with you tonight. I had my dad get me a ticket to this thing, just so I could see you. You looked beautiful; people went wild over you. I think the audience liked you best of all."

Kelly tried not to blush at the compliment. "The clothes and makeup made it easy," she explained. "I really felt beautiful."

"No, you looked beautiful yesterday, too," Alex said, expertly leading her around the dance floor.

Kelly didn't know what to say. She wasn't used to such outright compliments, but somehow, Alex made them sound genuine. She relaxed, enjoying his admiring glances.

"You're a great dancer," she said.

He grinned. "How come you're still here, anyway? I only expected to see you in the fashion show. What miracle made you stay—did you know I was waiting for you?"

"No, I mean, it wasn't a miracle—it was Paisley. She wanted to talk to Von Metzenberg about her dress designs, and," she confessed, "I wanted to see the ball."

"Like Cinderella, huh?" Alex said.

"How did you know—" She gazed at him in surprise. "I kept thinking to myself that I was like Cinderella at the ball. I couldn't bear the thought of going home." She laughed lightly. "I'm not supposed to be here, you know. I could get in trouble, wearing Clyde's dress . . ."

"Forget Clyde," Alex said flirtatiously. "He's not your prince tonight."

With unaccustomed ease, Kelly flirted back. "And I suppose you are?"

"Prince Alex, at your service." Alex bowed formally, then swept Kelly away, twirling her expertly among the other dancers.

Kelly was glad she had the Chinese slippers on. Throbbing feet would have spoiled the romance of dancing with Alex, and in flats, Kelly was the perfect height for this kind of dancing. Her head came just above Alex's shoulder as he held her close, and she felt protected in his arms.

He whirled her in a series of breathtaking turns. *It's turning into a beautiful night after all,* she thought.

A woman dressed in peacock blue, trailing matching feathers, leaned over as she danced by. "You were marvelous, dear," she said to Kelly, tapping her on the arm. "Stunning."

"Thank you." Kelly giggled. It was only the first of many compliments; every few minutes someone else would stop to say hello to Kelly, but she had forgotten her worries about being discovered; everyone seemed to enjoy having the models out on the dance floor. She glanced over at Paisley struggling with Mr. Von Metzenberg; he was possibly the world's worst dancer. Yet Paisley was laughing and carrying on, flirting outrageously—and Von Metzenberg loved it, showing her off, stopping other couples to point out the "gorgeous young lady" he was with. *No one will dare criticize Paisley for being here,* Kelly thought; *not with Metzy in her pocket like that.* Relieved, Kelly relaxed completely.

"How's your photography going?" she asked Alex.

"Pretty good. But I have so much other schoolwork right now, I hardly get into the darkroom. They say junior year will be easier; your requirements are over with."

"You're a sophomore?" Kelly felt better; she had thought Alex was much older, but a college sophomore was only about nineteen years old— not so much older than she. "How old will you be when you graduate?"

"Twenty-one; I'm nineteen now."

"Nineteen," Kelly said, calculating rapidly. "Only three years older than me."

"I hope you're not into really older men. Are you?" Alex seemed genuinely concerned.

"Oh, no, I think nineteen is a perfect age," she blurted, and then blushed; when would she learn to be a little bit cool with a boy? She shouldn't just blab things like that all over the place.

But Alex never seemed to pick up on the dumb things she said. Instead he made her feel right at home. They chatted easily while they danced, and everything she found out about Alex suited her perfectly. And everything she said about herself seemed to be fine with him.

That's the difference between a high-school boy and a college man, she thought, bitterly comparing Alex to Eric. Eric couldn't deal with the fact that Kelly was a model, while Alex thought she was wonderful for working. Alex thought Kelly was smart to take advantage of her looks. He said he admired women who had careers of their own, who didn't always depend on someone else. Alex said his mother worked hard for charities, and he thought everyone should have a purpose in life.

Alex made it perfectly clear, from things he said and did, that he liked Kelly a lot. That was another difference between a college man like Alex and a kid like Eric. Eric couldn't seem to make up his mind whether he liked Kelly or not. Why should Kelly put up with that when someone like Alex was so clearly interested in her?

Kelly tossed her head defiantly as she danced. Who cared what Eric Powers thought about Kelly Blake. She didn't—not one bit. Compared to Eric, Alex Hawkins really *was* Prince Charming!

"Let's sit this one out," Alex said after their fourth dance.

"I'm not a bit tired," Kelly said, "but we can sit down if you'd like. Maybe I should check on Paisley and Metzy."

"Yeah—let's see which one is giving the other a harder time."

The table was littered with paper napkins, each napkin covered with sketches of very Paisley-looking dresses. As Kelly and Alex approached, they caught Von Metzenberg covering a wide yawn. Kelly decided to give the older man a chance to get away in case Paisley was bothering him.

"Great party, Mr. Von Metzenberg," Alex said politely. "I hope you're enjoying yourself, sir."

"I hope we aren't keeping you from your guests," Kelly added.

"I *should* circulate now—as host, I should greet these people. . . ." He rose, pushing his chair back noisily.

"I'll come with you," Paisley offered, leaping instantly to Von Metzenberg's side.

"That's hardly necessary," he insisted. "I would rather go alone."

"Oh, I'm not going to let you out of my sight," Paisley teased, grabbing his arm. She draped herself over Von Metzenberg, hanging on for dear life. Then she suddenly turned pale; her eyes bulged, and her knuckles, where they grasped Von Metzenberg's arm, turned white.

"What? What is it?" Kelly asked, alarmed. "Are you sick?"

"Meg," Paisley gasped, "and Clyde."

Paisley lurched, fastening herself onto Kelly's arm. Without another word, she yanked Kelly off her feet, pulling her under the table.

"Paisley, get up this instant," Von Metzenberg ordered, his face red as he bent under the table. "This is preposterous."

"Are you crazy?" Kelly whispered to Paisley, prying her friend's fingers off her arm. "We can't sit under this table!"

"What's going on?" Von Metzenberg demanded.

Paisley hissed at him in a stage whisper: "It's Clyde—with Meg Dorian. They're heading this way—if they see us we're dead!"

Kelly's heart sank. Meg and Clyde—what a catastrophe. "But I thought," she said weakly, "I thought Metzy would protect us, that Clyde wouldn't mind our being here with him."

"I panicked," Paisley said. "My heart is thumping so fast I can hardly breathe."

"I'm getting up," Kelly said. "Metzy will explain to Clyde about the dresses." She tried to pull Paisley up with her. "Come on, Paisley, before they get to the table. If we don't get up now, we never will."

"With Meg out there? No way," Paisley wailed. She tugged at the tablecloth, pulling it down farther to cover them as Meg and Clyde drew closer. "I'm in enough trouble with Meg Dorian. I was late to shoots twice this week because I was out dancing the night before—with a man Meg detests! I can't cross her again. You don't know what Meg is like, Kelly. If she catches us, I guarantee it—neither of us will ever model again!"

Eleven

Kelly was mortified. Alex had seen her acting like a child—diving under a table to hide! Yet she couldn't get up; Meg would kill her for being there, and Clyde Mason would have a fit. She saw now that Von Metzenberg couldn't save them; he wouldn't protect them once he found out they didn't have Clyde's permission to wear the dresses. No, Von Metzenberg would probably expose them to Meg and Clyde; adults always stuck together.

Von Metzenberg would probably deliver some humiliating lecture about acting responsibly, and all the people who had praised Kelly would stare at her as if she were a freak. Alex would be embarrassed and pretend he wasn't with her. She'd lose her modeling career, and her parents— they'd never forgive her! Her father would walk around the house, grim and silent, for weeks, too angry to yell. Her mother would dissolve into tears, moaning about how Kelly had ruined her own future, her chance to go to college, her chance to be someone.

It was a total disaster.

Above her head, Kelly heard a round of kisses and pats on the back as everyone congratulated everyone else: Clyde on his successful new fashions, Meg on her beautiful models, Von Metzenberg on the tremendous response to the Children's Fund. Then she heard Alex introduce himself to Clyde and Meg as Sherwood Hawkins's son.

"Then you're no stranger to the fashion industry, Alex," Meg commented. It sounded like everyone except Kelly knew who Alex's father was; he must be even more important than Kelly realized.

Alex, sounding completely cool and collected, answered Meg, "Not a stranger at all. It's nice to finally meet you, Meg. Ah, would you like to dance?"

As if startled by the invitation, Meg laughed lightly. "Actually, I thought we might all have a drink together, to celebrate the occasion."

They heard a chair being pulled out, and Meg's feet grazed Kelly's side as she pulled her chair in. Kelly cowered, doubled-up beneath the table, shuffling as far away from Meg as possible and holding her breath. Bless Alex for trying to get Meg away from the table! Too bad it hadn't worked.

With her eyes shut, Kelly prayed that Meg and Clyde would go away. Paisley huddled close to Kelly, cringing as Meg and Clyde pulled their chairs close together, making themselves comfortable.

"Clyde, darling, have a drink," Meg offered.

Kelly felt hopeless. Alex couldn't keep asking Meg to dance, and how would he get rid of Clyde? The girls were stuck; if anyone else sat down, there would be absolutely no room for all those feet, plus Kelly and Paisley, underneath the table.

It was terrifying enough to think what Meg and Clyde would say when they discovered Kelly and Paisley wearing the exclusive dresses; but it would be unbelievably humiliating to be found hiding underneath a table at an important formal affair! Kelly squirmed; she could never live down the disgrace.

Paisley's designing career would be ruined before it even got started. Clyde would never look at her drawings now.

Meg's leg kicked out and Kelly pulled to one side. She kept picturing Meg's astonished face when she and Paisley crawled out from under the table. She also imagined the furious tongue-lashing she would get in public. Of course, Kelly would never model again. Even if someone, somewhere—in some unknown agency in some unknown small town—had never heard of the incident, Kelly would be too embarrassed to show her face in the modeling world after this. No, discovery now would mean the end; she would never live it down.

Paisley made a muffled gagging sound, trying to hold back an attack of hysterical giggles. *Oh, no, anything but that,* Kelly silently pleaded. Tears gathered in Paisley's eyes; she was seconds away from an explosion. Kelly turned her head, trying not to look. Giggles were contagious, especially in a tense situation—and this was one tense situation.

Kelly reached outside the tablecloth and punched Alex's leg, just above the ankle, in a desperate signal for help. *Rescue us*, she silently begged. *Please get them out of here!*

Above them, glasses tinkled and she could hear Meg's perplexed voice: "Why won't you two sit down?"

"I, uh," Alex stuttered. "Uh, Mr. Von Metzenberg was just saying how much he'd like to speak to my father—and, uh, take Mr. Mason with him!"

"I believe I spoke to your father, Alex," Clyde answered pleasantly.

"Yes, but he, ah, he especially wanted to talk to you *again*," Alex insisted. "About business. It's very important—some brilliant new merchandising idea . . ."

"Business can wait," Clyde insisted. "Working hours are over, okay?"

Kelly's heart sank. She might as well give up now. With a sigh of defeat, she lifted the tablecloth a few inches and peered at Alex's ankles, preparing to get up.

Frantically, Alex signaled for her to get back down. She gave him a look of despair. Von Metzenberg, glancing down, stared into Kelly's face. She felt like crying, it was such a disaster, but to her amazement, Von Metzenberg began to grin. Imagine him finding her situation funny, when she felt totally pathetic.

"What's that smile for?" Clyde said suspiciously. "Is Hawkins up to something big I should know about?"

"Hawkins?" Von Metzenberg said innocently. "I don't know about Woody's plans."

"Maybe I should speak to him again. Merchandising, eh?" Clyde shifted in his chair.

Grinning even wider now, Von Metzenberg winked at Kelly as she hastily dropped the tablecloth back into place. "I know nothing, Clyde, I assure you, but Woody's ideas are almost always winners . . ."

Kelly could have hugged Von Metzenberg for helping after all. Of course, she realized, it would be pretty embarrassing for him to explain why he'd allowed the girls to hide in Clyde's designs.

"Look, I just sat down," Clyde complained. "It can wait."

"Humor me," she heard Von Metzenberg answer. Then a chair scraped back and Clyde's feet withdrew from under the table.

"Well, time for that dance," Alex said brightly, pulling Meg's chair out.

"I hardly think . . ." Meg began, but Alex cut her off. "My favorite song," he cried. "I have to dance to this number—especially with you. I . . . I think you're fascinating."

Meg laughed, as if humoring Alex for his understandable crush on her, and their feet disappeared.

"They're gone," Kelly said, breathing a sigh of relief. At once, Paisley burst out laughing and Kelly, unable to stop herself, exploded into wild giggles.

"Too close," Paisley gasped. "I thought we'd never make it out alive."

"And Meg wouldn't budge," Kelly said, wiping a tear off her cheek. "She didn't want to dance with Alex—she must think he's insane!"

It was stuffy and hot beneath the table, and Kelly's back ached from bending over. Her laughing fit over, she shuffled to one side and peered cautiously from beneath the tablecloth. "If we go now, we can get out without them seeing us. We have to head for the main doors—Meg is dancing in front of the curtains."

They dissolved into another round of giggles. "Okay," Paisley finally said, taking a few deep breaths. "Ready."

Ignoring the astonished looks of the people at the next table, Kelly and Paisley scooted out from under the table and, still bent over, scurried toward the main doorway. Kelly stifled laughter; they were almost home free!

"Wait," Paisley cried, "what about Vanessa?"

"Oh, no," Kelly yelped, screeching to a halt just outside the doorway. Clinging together, the two girls turned to their left, fully expecting Vanessa to be standing in the same place, laughing with the same people they had seen her with earlier.

No one was there. "That was hours ago," Kelly realized. "She's somewhere else by now."

"Help," Paisley said. "I almost had a heart attack."

Sprinting the last few feet down the hallway, the girls raced around the corner, flinging themselves into the dressing area off the main hallway.

Kelly practically tore her dress off her body, tossing it anywhere while she scrambled through her bag for her jeans and top. Her heart didn't stop pounding until she finally had her own clothes back on.

"Whew," she exhaled loudly, collapsing onto a couch. "What a relief!"

While Paisley got into her own clothes, Kelly picked up the discarded evening gown, smoothed out the wrinkles as best she could, and went to hang it on the rack.

The rack was gone.

The dress hung limply from Kelly's hand as she stared in confusion. Maybe she had forgotten where the rack was. She whirled, searching every corner. But the dressing room was almost empty now, and there was no place to hide a rack of dresses. The rack was definitely gone.

The blood drained from her face; she felt light-headed.

"Paisley," she whispered, barely able to get a sound out, "the dresses are gone."

Paisley finished pulling on her high leather boots before looking up. "What's gone?" She lifted her evening gown by the straps, satisfied that it was in acceptable condition. "Great—I didn't rip a thing. No one will ever know."

Kelly grabbed her by the shoulders. "Listen to me—the rack is gone! The dresses aren't here—we're done for!"

Paisley finally looked around the room. "Oh, the rack—it is gone," she said vaguely. "Oh, well." She shrugged.

Kelly collapsed onto the couch. "But Vanessa was here," she cried. "You said Vanessa was still here . . ."

"She is," Paisley insisted. "Those are her books and things, over on that table. Vanessa won't go home until the ball is over, believe me."

"Well, good, but—the rest of the dresses aren't here," Kelly sputtered. "We have to get these back on the rack with the other dresses before

Vanessa or Clyde finds out they're missing. But the rack isn't in here. I don't know where it is."

"Take it easy." Paisley touched up her makeup, putting another coat of mascara on her pale lashes, staring into a pocket mirror. "They must have sent a man to pick up the rack. You know, in a van or something." Paisley avoided Kelly's eyes.

"A man?" she repeated.

"Well, yeah. Vanessa couldn't exactly wheel the rack from the hotel all the way to Clyde's showroom by herself, could she? They must have had a van."

Kelly's mouth fell open. "But then it wouldn't matter whether or not Vanessa was here," she said, appalled. "If they were sending a van for the dresses, Vanessa had nothing to do with the rack—and you knew it."

"I didn't *know*," Paisley said. "I'm just saying now that that's probably what's happened—they must have sent a man around with a van to pick up the rack. It just seems logical."

Kelly cradled her head between her hands. Suddenly she had a headache. "But you said all along—as long as Vanessa was still here, we were safe. You said as long as we got the dresses back before Vanessa went home, no one would know. Naturally, I thought Vanessa and the rack were connected somehow. Why wouldn't I think that?"

Paisley finished a few final adjustments to her clothes. "Really, Kelly," she said, annoyed, "how should I know why you think anything? I never *said* that about the rack; I don't control things any more than you do."

"But you led me to believe that," Kelly protested.

"I didn't lead you anywhere. Since when do I tell you what to do? I'm not your mother, I don't give orders. We both thought we'd have some fun and wear the dresses to the ball, that's all."

"How can you act so innocent!" Kelly stared at her in distress. "It *was* your idea, Paisley. I know I agreed to it, but you made it sound so harmless. You said the rack would still be here."

"Don't whine at me," Paisley snapped, though Kelly hadn't been whining. "I can't stand people whining at me."

"Well, I can't stand people tricking me, and it's the second time tonight you've done that."

"It is not."

"You never wanted to 'have fun,' as you put it; you wanted to show Metzy your designs, and get him to talk to Clyde about you. That's all you wanted—you didn't care about me, or the trouble I could get into. You didn't think of me as a friend that you wanted to go to a party with—you just wanted to use me, the way you accused me of using you! You haven't meant a word you said, and I thought we were friends. I don't think you know anything about friendship!"

"I do know about friendship, and I also know about business," Paisley retorted. "And I know when to mix the two. You didn't do anything I didn't do; we would both have been in the same amount of trouble, so don't accuse me of tricking you. One thing has nothing to do with another—I did too want to go to the ball with you, as a friend; but that doesn't mean I couldn't do a little business at the same time."

"You're crazy!" Kelly yelled. "Can't you see what you did wrong?"

"No, I don't see that I did anything wrong.

And besides, you promised to help me. So you were in it just as much as I was; you promised to get Metzy to talk to me."

"But only because I thought we could get the dresses back in time," Kelly said, totally exasperated.

"But we did," Paisley said, "we did get them back in time. Vanessa is still here. Just leave the dresses in here; when she comes in to get her stuff she'll see them and take them with her."

Kelly was astounded. "But the rack is gone. Vanessa will see the dresses that *we* wore tonight, and know that we were here when we shouldn't have been. What was the point of all that sneaking around if she was going to find out anyway?"

"I don't know, Kelly," Paisley said crossly, "but you didn't mind sneaking, did you? So don't act so superior, as if you never did anything wrong in your life."

Kelly groaned. "You don't see at all," she said. "We can't leave these dresses here for Vanessa; we were supposed to have them back ages ago. We might as well walk right out and hand them to her in the middle of everything, and admit we wore them all night."

Paisley hoisted her huge shoulder bag, settling it around her distinctive shawl. "Well, that would be stupid. If that's what you want to do, go ahead, but leave me out. I intend to leave my dress here, where Vanessa will find it."

"You'll ruin everything," Kelly cried, "don't you see? Oh, this is hopeless!"

There was a knock at the door, and Kelly looked up to find Alex cautiously leaning into the room. "Are you okay? Did anyone see you?"

"There—Alex is here," Paisley said, as if that fixed everything. "So I'm leaving—I'm meeting a friend at a club way downtown. See you, Kelly."

"We haven't decided anything . . . You can't go . . ."

But Paisley went, unfazed by Kelly's distress.

"What gives?" Alex walked into the room. "No one caught you, did they? You should have seen me, dragging poor Meg around the dance floor. I was afraid you didn't have time to get back yet, so I kept her out there for every dance. Who knows what I said to her; I was acting like a lunatic."

Kelly began to cry; she tried to pretend she wasn't, but Alex saw through her. And once she started, she couldn't stop.

"I'm sorry," she managed between sobs. "It's mostly anger . . . I'm so mad, and frustrated . . . How could she, I thought . . ."

Alex didn't say anything, just sat next to her and handed her his ironed handkerchief.

"Go ahead, use it," he said lightly. "You can keep it."

"I hate to use someone else's handkerchief," Kelly said through her tears, and laughed thinly. "It's so gross." She blew her nose, not even minding how awful it sounded, because Alex was laughing along with her.

Alex made her feel as if it was all right for her to cry. *He's someone I can really be friends with,* Kelly decided.

"I don't know what to do," she said when she had stopped crying. "I made a mess of things."

Alex listened patiently.

"Paisley was right, Alex. No one made me do it. I wanted to go to the party tonight; I wanted to have an adventure. But we're still in trouble and I can't take it—I guess I'm not as brave as I pretended to be. I'm so scared. I wish I could just walk out, like Paisley did, but I can't."

"Don't be so hard on yourself," Alex said. "Anyone would have been tempted. Anyway, I admire your nerve—it took guts to crash the ball. And don't forget," he added with a nice smile, "you were trying to help a friend."

"I did want to help Paisley," she admitted. "I wish I was more daring. I just couldn't resist a little adventure tonight. I felt like someone else in those clothes, with this wild hair and all that makeup on. I guess it can be dangerous, dressing up and acting like someone else."

"Everyone needs to have adventures," Alex said sympathetically.

"But I really hate the way Paisley just walked out of here. She didn't even think it was wrong to leave me stranded! And it *was* wrong; I would never do that to her. She really took advantage of me—I feel so stupid. I should have known better; I liked her!" Kelly sniffed. "I don't know, maybe she thought I could handle it better. Maybe she thought I could just walk out, too."

"Boy, I hope you're never a lawyer." Alex grinned. "You see both sides of every argument, don't you?"

Kelly laughed. "I've always been like that if I think about something long enough," she said. "But I have a temper, too. You should hear some of the mean things I've said to my mom."

"Me, too," Alex said.

"You? I don't believe it." Kelly searched Alex's clear gray eyes, but he wasn't teasing. "I don't believe you'd ever be mean to anybody."

"Well, not mean on purpose," he said, "not usually, anyway."

"I feel so much better, talking to you. You really get me talking—I could go on and on."

"I like to hear you talk about yourself," Alex said. "I feel like I know lots about you already."

"Me, too," Kelly said. "It's really nice to feel so comfortable with someone." Alex moved closer. Then he kissed her, and it was so nice—a gentle, soft sort of kiss. Kelly felt like kissing him forever, it seemed so natural, but then she surprised herself by jumping up suddenly.

Things are happening too fast, she thought. She hadn't expected to see Alex at all tonight, and here he was kissing her, listening to her confess her feelings. Yet she trusted Alex enough to feel sure that he would be the one to help her out.

Twelve

"We've got to do something about these dresses," Kelly reminded Alex, hoping he didn't think she was ignoring the fact that he had kissed her.

"Not that it's your problem," she added quickly. "I didn't mean that. It's my problem."

"I have an idea," Alex said, in a tone that told her he considered it his problem, too. "You don't want to leave the dresses here because Vanessa will know you took them when you shouldn't have."

"Right. And she'll tell Clyde, and he'll tell Meg."

"So secrecy is our biggest worry." Alex closed his eyes briefly. "Okay—I know what we'll do. Come on."

Kelly scooped up the dresses, stuffing them as neatly as possible into her big bag. "Where are we going?"

"To the showroom," Alex said. "Wait here. I'll make sure the coast is clear to the elevator—we don't want anyone catching us now, when we're so close to getting away with it, right?"

"Right."

Alex leaned down and kissed her again. When she opened her eyes, he was already gone, hurrying to the elevator.

With Alex to help her, Kelly began to relax. She felt like a private eye, or a spy, in a television show. Alex made everything exciting again, and she was almost sorry she had admitted to being scared before.

"Okay," he whispered, motioning for her to make a dash for the elevator while he held the door open. "Hurry!"

The elevator doors closed behind them. They were safe! *That is, as long as no one is lurking in the lobby*, Kelly thought.

"I'll check out the lobby before you get off," Alex said, as if reading her mind. "Just in case Meg or Clyde is standing there."

"Metzy," Kelly suddenly said. "Whatever happened to Metzy?"

Alex looked at her in surprise. "I forgot all about him."

Kelly giggled. "You sent him with Clyde, to talk to your father! Did your father really want to talk to Clyde?"

"No." Alex grinned. "My father doesn't even like Clyde Mason; he only said hello to him tonight to be polite. He sure didn't want to spend the evening with him."

"But you told Clyde your father really wanted to talk to him about business."

"Don't worry about it; my father thinks I'm

crazy, anyway. He won't notice one more weird thing I've done."

"And you don't mind him thinking that?"

"He thinks all kids are crazy," Alex said. "Don't everybody's parents think that?"

"I guess sometimes they do," Kelly said. They laughed together.

"Sure—sometimes you have to use that to your advantage." Alex bent and kissed her quickly on the lips, as the elevator doors slid open. He held one door and quickly scanned the lobby. "Coast is clear. Let's go find my car, okay?"

"Okay," Kelly said happily. She had a feeling she would follow Alex Hawkins anywhere tonight. "Alex, what if the showroom is closed, locked up? We're not going to break in, are we?"

"Break in? I hadn't thought of that," Alex admitted. He grinned slyly. "You're not afraid of doing something illegal, are you? Since your father's a cop I figured you must be a rebel; you know, really strict parents, so you go wild in revenge."

"It's not like that," Kelly protested. "My parents aren't too strict. Mostly we get along fine; just the usual screaming fights now and then, chiefly about my sister, Tina." Kelly shrugged. "I'm not the rebel type."

"That's okay," Alex said, but Kelly had a feeling he was slightly disappointed.

"I don't do *everything* my parents want me to do," she felt compelled to say. "I have plenty of fun."

"I bet you do." Alex smiled down at her. "Maybe we could have fun together."

Alex's car was a sleek new Datsun 300ZX. Kelly gaped as the garage attendant got out and handed Alex the keys. No one she knew had a car like that! Silvery gray on the outside with a black leather interior, it gleamed under the lights. Alex handed a generous tip to the driver, then held the door open while she climbed in. It was a tight squeeze for her long legs until Alex showed her how to adjust the seat so she would have more room.

"This car is fantastic," Kelly said, nestling into the smooth leather seat, admiring the shiny dials and gadgets covering the dashboard.

"It's not what I wanted," Alex admitted as they pulled away. "My parents surprised me with it. I wanted a four-wheel-drive Jeep, or a truck—equipment for a photographic safari in Africa. I was supposed to go last summer. Instead, I got this car and a big lecture about taking business more seriously. I spent the summer in one of my father's factories, learning the fashion industry from the ground up. What a bore."

"But if you really wanted to go to Africa, why didn't you trade this car in for a Jeep, or just save your own money and go, anyway?"

"I'm not a rebel, either," Alex said.

"But you said photography really matters to you. Couldn't you tell your father you'd rather pay your own way and do what you really wanted?"

"And risk losing my trust fund?"

"Your trust fund—is that an inheritance?"

"You could call it that. It's money set aside for me, but controlled by my father. He could have it stopped any time he wants. I'm at his mercy."

Kelly watched the city streets slide by her window. She had never known anyone rich enough to have a trust fund, or to receive a car as luxurious as Alex's as a present. His life must be completely different from hers; she couldn't imagine parents who didn't worry about money all the time.

"This is it," Alex announced, parking the car outside a nondescript building. "Seventh Avenue—the heart of the garment industry."

"It doesn't look like much of a showroom." Kelly frowned; she had expected something like a department store, with fancy awnings and beautiful clothes on display in the windows. She had never been to a designer's showroom before. "Are you sure this is the right place?"

Alex took her arm and walked her toward a dark alley. For a moment she was afraid, and she pulled back, unwilling to go down a dark alley with anyone, even someone she instinctively trusted as much as she trusted Alex.

He laughed. "The freight entrance," he said, pointing to a pair of double doors. "The elevator goes right to the showroom. Come on."

As they reached the freight elevator, the doors slid open, revealing two men in dark work clothes standing inside. Kelly's impulse was to run, but Alex had a firm grip on her arm and she couldn't budge an inch. The men got off the elevator, eyeing her and Alex suspiciously.

"You looking for something, bud?" the older man said.

"Yes, sir, I am," Alex answered politely. "A rack of dresses—Clyde Mason's dresses, going to his showroom."

The older man looked at his companion. Obviously, neither of them believed Alex, and Kelly felt indignant. What did they think she and Alex were, a pair of professional dress thieves? She giggled, partly out of nervousness, and the younger man's eyes narrowed, watching her carefully.

"I'm Alex Hawkins," Alex announced boldly. "Maybe you've heard of my father, Woody Hawkins. You know—the Woody Hawkins who owns half of Seventh Avenue?"

The two men stiffened. "So what?" the younger man said. "Who cares who you are?"

"I think you'll care very much. Show them the dresses, Kelly."

Kelly took the wrinkled dresses out of her bag, shaking them out to their full lengths.

"These are two of Clyde Mason's exclusive designs," Alex said, in the same polite tone of voice. "They were supposed to be on that rack you just delivered to Clyde's showroom."

"What is this?" The young man stepped toward them threateningly, and Kelly drew back, afraid of an ugly scene. This wasn't at all what she had expected—though she had no idea of what she *had* expected.

"I don't know how you got those dresses," the young man snarled, "but you better not threaten me. Maybe you stole them, and you want to steal more, but . . ."

Alex laughed. "No, it isn't me who's in trouble here," he said easily. "I'm afraid it's you."

"What are you talking about?" The young man was really angry now, and Kelly worried that Alex didn't know what he was doing. She had thought they could quietly replace the dresses without anyone noticing—she hadn't anticipated this kind of trouble.

"I know you just picked up a rack from the

Waldorf-Astoria Hotel to bring over here," Alex said. "Weren't you supposed to get *all* the dresses? They're very valuable, you know. Well, these two got left behind. Sloppy work, wouldn't you say? I don't suppose Clyde will be too happy to find these gowns missing in the morning. I suppose he'll feel that he has to fire the men responsible, especially if Woody Hawkins agrees."

"We did our job," the older man protested. "I don't know where those dresses came from, but we did our job right."

Alex pried the dresses from Kelly's hand; she was so bewildered she couldn't move.

"I'm sorry," Alex told the men, "but you didn't do your job right. You'd need these two dresses for that, wouldn't you?"

"What are you after?" the young man demanded. The older man just looked frightened. "What do you want from us?"

Alex acted totally surprised. "Want from you? I don't want anything. I'm offering you something, a chance to keep your jobs. You can thank Kelly, here—she thought it would be a shame to have you fired for a simple oversight like leaving these expensive dresses behind. Didn't you, Kelly?"

"Well, I wouldn't want anyone to get fired," she said anxiously. "Really, I don't want any trouble at all."

"Right. So Kelly begged me to bring these dresses over here, so whoever was responsible wouldn't be in any trouble." He handed the dresses to the older man.

"Thanks," the man said, exchanging a look of relief with his partner. "That was fair of you, miss."

Kelly blushed. "Don't thank me," she said guiltily, finally understanding what Alex was doing.

"No, I do thank you," the older man insisted. "And you, too, son—thanks a lot. We'll get these dresses right upstairs. Mr. Mason would be pretty mad to find them gone in the morning—I guess you saved my job at that."

The young man turned his back, holding the elevator doors open until his companion was safely inside.

"Thanks again," the older man called as the doors shut.

"Whew," Alex said as soon as they were gone. "Did you see that young guy's face? I thought he was going to slug me, for sure."

"I'm so glad it's over with," Kelly said in relief. "It was pretty tense—and you really caught me off guard with that story."

"You were great—they loved you," Alex said. "A beautiful angel of mercy."

"But I didn't do anything. I didn't really save their jobs."

"They thought you did—did you see how grateful the old guy was? I really had him worried. I'll bet he sweats all the way home, thinking about his close call."

"I'm so relieved," Kelly said. "Alex—you saved my life."

Alex chuckled. "You sure create excitement. What an evening!"

"I didn't make the excitement, you did," Kelly insisted.

They climbed back into the car. "Where to?" Alex said. "I feel great. And you—you rescued those guys from big trouble."

"But I'm the one who was in trouble, not those two men," Kelly said uneasily. "You couldn't really get them fired, could you?"

"Hey, I know it was sort of a dirty trick," Alex said, "but it didn't hurt anyone. Look, when you're dead wrong, you have to put the shoe on the other foot. Those guys were plenty suspicious when we showed up with the dresses. If I hadn't turned the tables on them, they might have called the cops."

"I guess you're right—and I really appreciate it, Alex. But that old man was so scared, I felt sorry for him."

"You're a sweet kid," Alex said. "So where to now—dancing?"

Kelly hesitated. It would be wonderful to go to a rock club with Alex, but it was late and she had told her mother she'd be home right after the benefit. She really ought to call her mother right now, but Alex would think she was a baby if she did that.

Maybe I should just go dancing, and risk it with Mom, Kelly thought. *She can't be too angry when she finds out who I was with. And wouldn't Jennifer be jealous to find out I'd gone dancing with a gorgeous, rich college boy like Alex! Even Eric might be jealous. But that's no way to think*, she told herself sternly.

"If you don't mind . . ." she said hesitantly. "I'd really love to go dancing with you, Alex, but it's pretty late. I should just go home to Jersey."

"No problem—I'll drive you there. Where to?"

"You'll drive me? Great! I live in Franklyn. Do you know where it is?"

"I think so. You can show me the turns once we're near there." Alex smiled, deftly swung the car into a U-turn, and headed toward the Lincoln Tunnel, which would take them to New Jersey. For a while they drove in silence.

"Is your father really that well known?" she finally asked, glad to change the subject. "As well known as Clyde Mason?"

"Everyone in the industry knows him. And don't be too impressed by Clyde Mason. He's just a designer, and my father hires hundreds of designers, for everything from lipsticks to table-cloths to evening gowns and sneakers. Designers aren't that great. They have assistants, you know, and half the time, the assistants come up with the ideas, and the designers put their own names on them."

"I didn't know that. I thought a designer did all his own work. Does that mean if Paisley became a designer, she'd just give her designs away?"

"She'd get paid for it," Alex answered. "But yes, that could happen. Or she could get lucky and make it on her own, with her own name. Usually that takes years, though; she'd probably start by working for someone else. It's a tough business, Kelly, like any other."

"I'm sorry you told me. I liked it better not knowing how things really are. Sometimes I think you can know too much. It spoils the fun."

"You're wonderful." Alex smiled at her, delighted. "You're different from most girls I know. You know the type, typical debutantes—wild, and bored with everything. You're not bored with anything, are you?"

"Not bored," Kelly said. "There're so many things I've never done yet."

"And you're innocent. I like that, too. It's nice

to be with someone who's doing things for the first time."

"I'm not so innocent," Kelly protested. "Maybe I haven't been around as much as your rich friends, but I'm not out of it."

"Don't get touchy. I liked your wearing that dress tonight so you wouldn't miss the ball. I admire a person who breaks the rules sometimes, maybe because I'm usually afraid to break them."

Alex watched the road thoughtfully, and Kelly almost felt sorry for him. She'd never met a "poor little rich boy" before, and even though she wasn't nearly as daring or brave as Alex seemed to think, it pleased her to let him think she was. *I want him to admire me*, she realized.

At the next red light, Alex pulled her close and kissed her.

"You really are special," he breathed. "You taste brand-new."

Kelly liked his kisses, but his compliments confused her. He made such a big deal of her being fresh and innocent, when she wanted to be thought of as mature and confident; it was almost insulting. Sure, it was nice to be fussed over, but she didn't like his acting as if he knew so much more than she did.

As if sensing her doubts, Alex released her and began driving again. She glanced at his profile, his hair lit like a golden halo by passing streetlights. He probably didn't mean to insult her; it wasn't his fault he had been around more than she had. He was fun and good-looking and rich; girls probably fought over him all the time. *I should thank my lucky stars a boy like that is interested in me*, she thought.

"You know, Kelly," he said quietly, "if you have

a problem, you could come to me for help. I'd like that. Like tonight; I could have told Clyde I insisted you dance with me, in that dress; he would have said it was okay. I could have fixed it with Meg Dorian, too."

Kelly turned to stare at him. "Then why did you let me act like such an idiot? Why did you let me hide under the table? And then why did we go through that scene with those two men? We could have gotten in big trouble—it might even have been dangerous."

"But it was fun," Alex answered, as if she had said something stupid. "I told you—I enjoy acting crazy once in a while."

"You're different than I thought," Kelly said slowly. "I thought you were more serious. I thought you weren't spoiled, that you worked hard for things you cared about, like your photography. I suppose that's just a game to you, too."

Alex flushed. "Don't ever say that. I am serious about it. No one wants me to be the artistic type; they never have—but it's in me to be creative. I'll show you my work sometime; you'll see that I have real talent. But I can't help the way I've been raised. I didn't ask to be born rich and overprotected. Should I apologize for liking to act a little crazy, for having some fun? Am I supposed to give the money away? Would that make you take me seriously?"

"No," Kelly admitted. "That wouldn't make any sense."

"Then don't judge me," he said. "I'd like to get to know you—why don't you give yourself a chance to get to know me? I'm not a bad guy."

His clear gray eyes pleaded with hers. She couldn't refuse his request, and she didn't want to. "I'd like to get to know you, too," she said sincerely.

Thirteen

They rode the rest of the way to Kelly's house in silence. Something was definitely happening between them, something that hadn't happened to Kelly before, and yet she felt calm and sure of herself. As they neared her street, Kelly sat up and began pointing out landmarks to Alex: her elementary school, the corner where she fell off her first two-wheeler. Alex laughed along with her stories, and she felt that she was sharing the best part of herself with him.

"Elmhurst Lane—my block—is the next cross street," Kelly pointed out as they turned a corner. "It's not much of a house," she said, at once embarrassed that her house might look small and ordinary to Alex, and at the same time pleased because her parents had worked so hard to make it attractive. Her home might not be a mansion, but the big trees surrounding the house gave it a protected, cozy look, and the newly painted shutters and window boxes were cheerful, even at night with only the streetlights shining on them. *It's a perfect kind of house to grow up in,* Kelly thought; *nothing too fancy, but warm and welcoming.* She hoped Alex would think so, too.

As Alex turned the car into Elmhurst Lane, Kelly looked over at Eric's big white house. She noted light shining through the kitchen windows.

The car had slowed at the corner, but now Alex revved up the motor and shifted gears; the noise was loud enough to attract plenty of attention. In fact, Kelly hoped her father wasn't working nearby—how embarrassing it would be if he gave Alex a ticket for disturbing the peace!

Accelerating quickly, Alex let out a wild yell and they burst away from the corner, racing up the street with an impressive roar.

Kelly couldn't help laughing. "We probably woke up the whole block!" she said.

Alex leaned close again. "You *are* fun," he said softly, then kissed her good night, a warm, lingering kiss this time. She smiled at him happily.

"I don't suppose you'd like to go out tomorrow?" he asked. "Brunch in the city? I could pick you up around eleven. How about it?"

"I'd love to!" Kelly didn't even think of disguising her enthusiasm until she saw the indulgent twinkle in Alex's eye. "I *always* love Sunday brunch in the city," she quickly added.

"Sure you do," Alex said. He gave her another quick kiss, and then Kelly grabbed her bag and jumped out of the car. It wasn't until she was standing on the sidewalk, waving as Alex noisily pulled away, that she realized she hadn't given him a chance to walk her to her front door!

She remained standing on the sidewalk for a moment, savoring the idea of her date with Alex on Sunday. *Just a casual brunch in the city,* she said silently, practicing the phrase for school on Monday, when all her friends would want to know about the charity ball. Just the usual celebrities, she would say easily, and then my date, Alex Hawkins—son of Woody Hawkins, the fashion industry magnate—then Alex and I ran his 300ZX into the city for brunch on Sunday; just the usual thing.

The front door to Eric's house opened, and surprise replaced her triumphant excitement. Could Jennifer still be at Eric's house? She realized she was standing alone on Eric's sidewalk, grinning like an idiot into the empty street. She flushed, and not just from embarrassment. In that instant she realized nothing had changed; despite the thrill of being with Alex, despite having a date with him for the next day, her heart still pounded at the thought of seeing Eric. *After all he put me through, I still have a crush on that impossible boy!*

"Kelly—is that you?"

Kelly jumped at the sound of Jennifer's voice.

"Oh, it's you. I thought it was Eric." Disappointment flooded through her. Jennifer was the last person she wanted to see.

Jennifer's arms were wrapped around a pile of books and notebooks. "Eric was just going to take me home. He's looking for his keys. I tried to wait for you, but it got so late."

"Oh? I'm sure your study date went fine without me," Kelly said coldly, hoping Jennifer caught her sarcasm. "You and Eric get a lot of work done?"

"Yeah, as a matter of fact, we did. But who cares about me! Come on, tell me, what was it like? How did you look? Who was there?"

"You couldn't care less," Kelly snapped.

"Kelly!" Jennifer took a step closer. "What's with you? Was it awful? Oh, no," she groaned, "you hated it. I'm sorry—I really thought you'd enjoy yourself tonight."

"I bet you did—I bet the only thing you could think about all night was how much fun I was having at the fashion show."

"That's right," Jennifer said in a puzzled voice. "I did think about you all night. Eric and I kept saying how lucky you were to be out—we both felt like wallflowers, home studying on a Saturday night. And Eric really had catching up to do—I never saw such messy, worthless notes in my life! But it works out perfectly. You can study with him all day tomorrow." She smiled in satisfaction.

"Me—tomorrow?" Kelly stared at Jennifer, baffled. "What about you? Why don't you want to study with Eric?"

Jennifer looked at her as though she were crazy. "I'm not the one in love with Eric Powers, remember? This whole evening was a setup for you. I waited and waited for you to get back. He must think I'm a real grind; I kept insisting we do one more chapter. I mean, I'll probably ace this test because of tonight, but I'm pretty sick of computers myself. Why were you so late? And who drove you home?"

Kelly couldn't say anything at first. Then she

suddenly wrapped her arms around Jennifer, books and all, and gave her a big hug.

"I'm such a dope," she cried. "I owe you a big apology, Jen—I'm so sorry!"

"What are you talking about?"

"All night, I thought you were plotting against me. Eric made that crack about me having better things to do tonight, and then you offered to study with him—I thought you stabbed me in the back, Jen. Oh, I'm a terrible friend. How could I ever doubt you?"

"Why would you think that?" Jennifer was shocked. "I've never been interested in Eric!"

"I know," Kelly said miserably, "but I wanted to spend time alone with Eric, and you got to do it instead. At the library yesterday, and then tonight."

"But I did it for you!"

"I know that now. But I got so jealous—I imagined you both calling me names, laughing at me . . ."

"Laughing at you! Kelly Blake, wake up. Eric and I admire you—we agreed on that tonight. He even said so."

"He did?" Kelly couldn't believe it. "But when the limo came for me, he looked disgusted."

"He was embarrassed," Jennifer explained. "What boy wouldn't feel put down when the girl he asks out gets into a limousine and drives away? He must have felt terrible. But I don't think he held it against you."

"Did he say anything about me?"

Jennifer bit her lip to keep from smiling. "I told him about our sixth-grade fashion show and how worried you were about tonight."

"You didn't, Jen, that's awful."

"He thought it was hilarious, and he really

understood how hard tonight was for you. Don't forget, I've known you forever, but Eric hasn't been here that long. He loved hearing about you as a little kid; he said he felt he knew you better now."

Alex had enjoyed hearing about her, too. "I guess it is important to know a lot about someone," Kelly said.

"I waited for you to show up all evening," Jennifer finished. "I can't believe you were thinking I stabbed you in the back."

"Me, either," Kelly said. "I hated thinking that about you! It's much nicer having a best friend again. You know, modeling might be bad for me. I never used to be so suspicious. Maybe I wasn't cut out for it. I can't handle juggling two lives."

"Look, Kelly," Jennifer said sternly. "It really hurts that you didn't trust me tonight. But don't go quitting modeling. You *were* made for this business. I guess the pressures and everything got to you more than they should, but don't even think about giving it up." Jennifer couldn't stay angry with Kelly for long. "Although," she said smiling, "you did look awfully nervous tonight, getting into that limo. I got the feeling you wanted to jump out."

"Part of me did," Kelly confessed. "Part of me was scared stiff."

"But the other part . . . ?"

"The other part was really excited. And being on the runway was terrific fun, once I got used to it. But I'm still confused; someone like Paisley Gregg knows this is exactly what she wants to be doing, while I'm worried about missing out on regular things, like study dates and track meets. She's so sure—I'm not sure of anything."

"But you're just starting," Jennifer reassured her. "Give it a chance. Anything worth having takes time; that's what my mom always says."

Anything worth having—Kelly wondered if that applied to boys. Maybe Eric just needed more time. But why waste *her* time wondering about it, when she knew Alex was interested in her right now?

"I feel so stupid for doubting you," Kelly said. "And I have so much more to tell you! Alex drove me home, and—"

"Alex?" Jennifer interrupted. "That college boy you met? He was at the benefit tonight?"

"He was the one in the car," Kelly said. "The Datsun."

"It sure makes a lot of noise! Did you have fun with Alex?"

"He was even handsomer tonight than I remembered, and he went to the benefit just to see me," Kelly said slowly. "He really knows how to flatter a girl. And he saved my career, too."

Quickly, she told Jennifer the story of how she and Paisley "borrowed" the dresses.

"I have a feeling Alex would do anything for me," Kelly finished. "But sometimes he makes me feel like I come from another planet."

"Do you like him or don't you?"

"It *was* exciting to be with him tonight. We did some crazy things." Kelly chuckled. "And it was romantic, too. We have a date for brunch tomorrow in the city." Then why was she afraid to say she liked him?

"Now I *am* impressed," Jennifer said. "He sounds terrific—maybe you should forget about Eric. Can I come over tomorrow to meet Alex? I'll tell you what I think of him."

"Sure—that would be fun. But we'll have to make it seem perfectly natural. You know, you could just drop by to return a sweater or something."

"Great!" Jennifer said. "I'll call you tomorrow morning first thing to figure out a plot."

"Then I'm forgiven?"

Jennifer frowned, then gave Kelly a quick smile. "You're forgiven," she said. "After all, I have to get a look at Alex, the mysterious stranger!"

Eric appeared on the porch, holding up his car keys. "You wouldn't believe where—" He stopped when he saw Kelly standing on the sidewalk with Jennifer. "Kelly!"

"Hi," Kelly said. "Guess I missed the study session."

"That's okay. How was the fashion show?" he asked.

"Tiring." She smiled, expecting that Eric, unlike Jennifer, would be satisfied with that answer.

"I'd like to hear more about it. I mean, I really hoped you'd make it over tonight. I was looking forward to seeing you."

"You were?" Kelly couldn't hide her surprise.

"Hey, you guys," Jennifer interrupted them. "I'm kind of cold. Eric, want to give me the keys and I'll wait in the car?"

"Oh . . ." Eric hesitated a moment, then gave her the keys. "Here they are, but I'll just be a minute."

Jennifer took the car keys and said, "I'll see you tomorrow, Kel."

Kelly waved and watched as Jennifer went

around to the driveway, where Eric's car was parked. Then she turned back to Eric.

He was watching her with a look that made her heart stop. "Sure I wanted to see you tonight," he said. "I like to talk to you."

"I didn't think you cared much what I did," she confessed. She had intended her tone to be light, but from the expression in Eric's eyes, she'd failed.

"I do care," he said simply. "I mean, I like you and I'm interested in what you do."

All thoughts of Alex fled from Kelly's mind, and she felt her old awkwardness with Eric returning. Did he mean he liked her *that* way? Or did he mean in a friendly way?

"It's hard for me to say this," Eric continued. "I wasn't going to say anything, but then it seemed stupid not to. Do you know what I mean?"

She hadn't any idea what he was talking about. "You mean you're interested in my modeling career?"

"No, no. I'm not explaining this right." Eric took a deep breath. He looked adorable, his hair tousled, his eyes dark with fatigue. He seemed at a total loss for words, and for some reason Kelly found this irresistibly sweet. *He's uncomfortable with me*, she realized; *he can't talk to me, either.* It cheered her up immeasurably.

"I've got a girlfriend," Eric blurted, "back in Yellow Springs, where we used to live. Clarissa Robbins. It's not that I was trying to hide anything . . ." He threw his hands out helplessly.

That was the one thing Kelly had never thought of to explain why Eric couldn't seem to get serious about her. She was speechless.

Fourteen

"I guess some of us wondered why you weren't dating anyone steadily." *Wondered*, Kelly thought; *I lay awake nights trying to figure you out, Eric Powers. But I never imagined this!*

"Are you serious?" she asked. "You and this, uh, Clarissa?" *How could you*, she wanted to scream at Eric. *How could you like someone with a dopey name like that?* She pictured ringlet curls, tons of lace, and sickeningly sweet perfume, then caught herself. She was being ridiculous; Eric would never like a girl like that. *And if he does*, she realized mournfully, *I won't make it any better by getting catty and angry.*

"She's terrific," Eric said. "Everybody likes her. She's one of those people that girls want for a best friend and boys want to date. Everyone likes her," he repeated.

"You said that," Kelly said dryly. She hoisted

her shoulder bag, getting ready to go home. A big knot had suddenly formed in her throat. "Well, it's been a long night, and Jennifer's waiting. . . ."

"Please, there's more," Eric said.

Kelly hesitated. "You don't have to explain to me." She wasn't sure she could handle any more confessions like this one. "I didn't ask for explanations."

"No, but I want to." Eric took another deep breath. "In case you were wondering why I didn't spend more time with you."

Kelly acted surprised. "Me? Why, I never thought—we didn't have that kind of relationship. You're a great guy, but we were both on the cross-country team and I know how messy that can get, when a guy and a girl have *too* much in common. I mean, I never . . ."

"I wanted to see you more often," he said firmly, catching her by surprise. "But I promised Clarissa not to get too involved with any girl here. She and I have known each other all our lives—everyone back home knows we're a couple. When my folks moved here, Rissa—that's her nickname—was pretty shook up. She didn't want to break up."

"Did you?" Kelly asked faintly. Her head was spinning with this unexpected information. What was Eric trying to do to her? She was tempted to tell Eric she had a boyfriend, a college boy, and she couldn't get involved, either.

"No, I didn't want to break up at the time," he admitted. "I lived in that town all my life—everyone knew me, I knew everyone. I had a place on the track team, the teachers all thought I was a good student. I'm a pretty quiet guy," he said, as if Kelly didn't know that already, "and I keep to myself. I didn't know how I'd ever fit in here. I guess I thought I needed Rissa as much as she said she needed me. I didn't want to be alone."

"No one wants to be alone." Kelly had lived in Franklyn all her life; she understood what he was talking about. How would she feel, leaving her friends behind, starting all over in a new high school?

"It's not easy breaking into the groups at school," she went on sympathetically. "And the teachers—they peg you right away. Everyone labels you. And if you're brand new, they can get the wrong idea. It's tough, I know."

Eric looked pleased at how well she understood his problem. "That's what I thought," he said. "Only it turned out okay. Coach likes me—that's the most important thing, and I'm doing well in school. I have great friends. Things have gone all right for me."

Kelly looked at him. *With your face*, she thought, *and that personality and your terrific build, why wouldn't things go all right for you?*

"That's great," was all she said.

"And that's how things stand," Eric continued. "I fit in here, and that means my old friends have become just that—old friends. I mean, I'll always like them and be glad to see them, but my life is here now. Only Clarissa doesn't see it that way."

"What are you telling me—you're going with her or you're breaking up with her?"

"Neither," Eric said. "I can't break up with her; she's begged me not to. But I told her she should date other guys, and that I had to be free to date other girls here, once in a while. I have to—my life is here." He paused. "And you're here."

Kelly thought her heart would drop out and fall to her feet. *After all this time—why now?* she thought wildly. *Now that there's Alex . . . If only I had more time . . .*

But she'd never needed time to decide how she felt about Eric, not from the first moment she saw him.

Eric seemed to take her silence for doubt. "Unless—" he said, "well—what would a girl like you want with me?"

"You're the school's track star," she cried, amazed that he could be so modest. *Don't give up now, Eric,* she said to herself. *Please, don't give up.* She took a deep breath and said aloud, "Actually, I always liked you."

It was out. It had taken tremendous courage, but now he knew.

"Look, Kelly, I'm a plain kind of guy. Seeing you tonight, all made up to look like—a movie star," he said, "was sort of overwhelming. And that limousine; that's where you belong. A guy like me, limos aren't my style. . . ."

"Well, what does that have to do with anything?" Kelly shook her head impatiently. "You know me, at least you should. I'm not fancy. I live right across the street, not in a mansion. You know my family; they're just like yours."

"I don't want you to look down on me or anything. I can't compete with your new life."

"I would never ask you to," she burst out.

Eric reached over and lightly stroked the back of Kelly's hand. She froze at his touch; her stomach fluttered, and she found herself unable to speak. They were both looking at their hands, watching as if hypnotized. After what seemed an eternity, he curled his fingers around hers, holding on tightly. Neither of them looked at the other's face; she held her breath.

Eric finally said, "Want to go out with me tomorrow? An early date, since there's school the next day," he added. "Maybe hamburgers and a movie in the afternoon?"

Two dates! Two dates in one day! "I'd love to," she said aloud.

Her mind clicked into gear: Alex was picking her up at eleven, brunch would last a couple of hours, movies started around two or four. She could spend the early afternoon with Alex and get back in time to spend the late afternoon with Eric.

Of course she had to work it so he didn't see Alex's car drive up or drop her off. That fancy Datsun; imagine what Eric would say after her speech! She had to keep the two boys apart, but how?

Jennifer, she thought. *Jennifer will help.*

Across the street the Blakes' door flew open and Kelly's mother—in her robe and slippers!—rushed across the front lawn.

"Kelly Blake! Is that you standing there? With me half out of my mind, worrying!"

"Uh, I've gotta go, Eric," Kelly said quickly. "Call me tomorrow morning—we'll work out the details . . ."

Her mother kept coming, right across the street. "I've been worried sick, young lady," she called. "I phoned Meg Dorian, but there was no answer. What are you doing out here, how did you get home?"

"Mother, please." Kelly grabbed her mother's

arm and pulled her toward their house. "You're not dressed."

"If your father was home . . ."

"Mom—I'm fine, see, all in one piece. A friend drove me home. The benefit was fabulous! Wait till I tell you about your favorite movie stars who were there!"

She turned at her front door. Eric was getting into his car; she heard Jennifer say something to him in a teasing voice. She could hear Eric's answering laugh before he slammed the door and started the motor.

Jen will get on me tomorrow for keeping her waiting, Kelly thought, but she knew Jennifer wouldn't really be mad. *Just wait until she hears what Eric told me!*

"What was it really like?" her mother asked as soon as they were in the house.

Kelly thought of the long evening: the excitement, the tears, her bleeding feet, the beautiful dresses she wore, the wild applause; and at the end of it all, Prince Charming—not one, but two Prince Charmings. Her eyes were shining as she answered.

"It was like a fairy tale," she said.

ABOUT THE AUTHOR

YVONNE GREENE was born in the Netherlands and emigrated to the United States as a young girl. At seventeen, she began a successful international modeling career, which she still pursues today. She has been featured on the pages of all the major American and European fashion magazines. Ms. Greene is also the author of two best-selling Sweet Dreams novels, *Little Sister* and *Cover Girl*, and *The Sweet Dreams Model's Handbook*.

THE GLAMOROUS, EXCITING WORLD OF FASHION MODELING COULD BE *YOUR* WORLD! *FIND OUT ABOUT IT*

Send *for your FREE copy of*

THE SWEET DREAMS MODEL'S HANDBOOK

by Yvonne Greene, author of
the *Kelly Blake, Teen Model* books
Fill out the coupon below and send it to:
Lee Enterprises
Sweet Dreams Model's Handbook
17111 S. Wallace
South Holland, IL 60473
Hurry—your coupon must be received by October 31, 1986.
Offer available while supplies last.

Please send me my free copy of
THE SWEET DREAMS MODEL'S HANDBOOK

Name: _____ Age: _____

Address: _____

City: _____ State: _____ Zip: _____

SWEET DREAMS are fresh, fun and exciting,—alive with the flavor of the contemporary teen scene—the joy and doubt of *first love*. If you've missed any SWEET DREAMS titles, from #1 to #100, then you're missing out on *your* kind of stories, written about people like *you*!

☐ 24460	P.S. I LOVE YOU #1 Barbara P. Conklin	$2.25
☐ 24332	THE POPULARITY PLAN #2 Rosemary Vernon	$2.25
☐ 24318	LAURIE'S SONG #3 Debra Brand	$2.25
☐ 24319	LITTLE SISTER #5 Yvonne Green	$2.25
☐ 24323	COVER GIRL #9 Yvonne Green	$2.25
☐ 24324	LOVE MATCH #10 Janet Quin-Harkin	$2.25
☐ 24832	NIGHT OF THE PROM #12 Debra Spector	$2.25
☐ 24291	TEN-BOY SUMMER #18 Janet Quin-Harkin	$2.25
☐ 24466	THE POPULARITY SUMMER #20 Rosemary Vernon	$2.25
☐ 24338	SUMMER DREAMS #36 Barbara Conklin	$2.25
☐ 24838	THE TRUTH ABOUT ME AND BOBBY V. #41 Janetta Johns	$2.25
☐ 24688	SECRET ADMIRER #81 Debra Spector	$2.25
☐ 24383	HEY, GOOD LOOKING #82 Jane Polcovar	$2.25
☐ 24823	LOVE BY THE BOOK #83 Anne Park	$2.25
☐ 24718	THE LAST WORD #84 Susan Blake	$2.25
☐ 24890	THE BOY SHE LEFT BEHIND #85 Suzanne Rand	$2.25
☐ 24945	QUESTIONS OF LOVE #86 Rosemary Vernon	$2.25
☐ 24824	PROGRAMMED FOR LOVE #87 Marion Crane	$2.25
☐ 24891	WRONG KIND OF BOY #88 Shannon Blair	$2.25
☐ 24946	101 WAYS TO MEET MR. RIGHT #89 Janet Quin-Harkin	$2.25

☐ 24992	TWO'S A CROWD #90 Diana Gregory		$2.25
☐ 25070	THE LOVE HUNT #91 Yvonne Green		$2.25
☐ 25131	KISS & TELL #92 Janet Quin-Harkin		$2.25
☐ 25071	THE GREAT BOY CHASE #93 Janet Quin-Harkin		$2.25
☐ 25132	SECOND CHANCES #94 Nany Levinso		$2.25
☐ 25178	NO STRINGS ATTACHED #95 Eileen Hehl		$2.25
☐ 25179	FIRST, LAST, AND ALWAYS #96 Barbara Conklin		$2.25
☐ 25244	DANCING IN THE DARK #97 Carolyn Ross		$2.25
☐ 25245	LOVE IS IN THE AIR #98 Diana Gregory		$2.25
☐ 25297	ONE BOY TOO MANY #99 Marian Caudell		$2.25
☐ 25298	FOLLOW THAT BOY #100 Debra Spector		$2.25
☐ 25366	WRONG FOR EACH OTHER #101 Debra Spector		$2.25
☐ 25367	HEARTS DON'T LIE #102 Terri Fields		$2.25
☐ 25429	CROSS MY HEART #103 Diana Gregory		$2.25
☐ 25428	PLAYING FOR KEEPS #104 Janice Stevens		$2.25
☐ 25469	THE PERFECT BOY #105 Elizabeth Reynolds		$2.25
☐ 25470	MISSION: LOVE #106 Kathryn Maris		$2.25
☐ 25535	IF YOU LOVE ME #107 Barbara Steiner		$2.25
☐ 25536	ONE OF THE BOYS #108 Jill Jarnow		$2.25
☐ 25643	NO MORE BOYS #109 White		$2.25
☐ 25642	PLAYING GAMES #110 Eileen Hehl		$2.25

Prices and availability subject to change without notice.

Sweet
Dreams

WINNERS

THIS EXCITING NEW SERIES IS ALL ABOUT THE THREE MOST ENVIED, IMITATED AND ADMIRED GIRLS IN MIDVALE HIGH SCHOOL: STACY HARCOURT, GINA DAMONE AND TESS BELDING. THEY ARE WINNERS—GOLDEN GIRLS AND VARSITY CHEERLEADERS—YET NOT EVEN THEY CAN AVOID PROBLEMS WITH BOYFRIENDS, PARENTS, AND LIFE.

☐ **THE GIRL MOST LIKELY (WINNERS #1) 25323/$2.25**

Stacy Harcourt is the captain of the varsity cheerleading squad, but she wants to break from her rigid, boring image as "Miss Perfect." But in doing so will she lose the friendship of Gina and Tess and the captainship of the squad? Or will she realize that maybe her "perfect" life wasn't so bad after all. 25323/$2.50

☐ **THE ALL AMERICAN GIRL (WINNERS #2)25427/$2.25**

Gina Damone has problems keeping up socially with the other cheerleaders because of her immigrant parents old-world attitudes. But when she begins dating All-American Dex Grantham his breezy disregard for her parents' rules makes her question his sincerity.

☐ **THE GOOD LUCK GIRL (WINNERS #3)   25644/$2.25**

Cute, cuddly Tess Belding is the first student from Midvale's vocational-technical program ever to make the cheering squad, but she's going to be benched unless she can pass her French midterm!